"HERE'S WHERE WE STRIP DOWN ..."

"We what?" she asked, as she moved up beside Fargo.

"Undress. Get your clothes off," Skye said, even as he began to peel his shirt from his powerful shoulders. He finished pulling his shirt free and began to fold it. "You going to get out of those clothes?"

"You're not joking, are you?" she said, watching his face.

"Would I joke about something like that? Now, you going to get out of those clothes on your own or do you want help?"

He smiled to himself as she began to toy with the buttons on her blouse, opening the top one to let high, round mounds push forward ...

Exciting Westerns by Jon Sharpe

THE TRAILSMAN
22

BORDER
ARROWS

by
Jon Sharpe

A SIGNET BOOK
NEW AMERICAN LIBRARY
TIMES MIRROR

PUBLISHER'S NOTE

This novel is a work of fiction. Names, characters, places, and incidents either are the product of the author's imagination or are used fictitiously, and any resemblance to actual persons, living or dead, events, or locales is entirely coincidental.

NAL BOOKS ARE AVAILABLE AT QUANTITY DISCOUNTS WHEN USED TO PROMOTE PRODUCTS OR SERVICES. FOR INFORMATION PLEASE WRITE TO PREMIUM MARKETING DIVISION, THE NEW AMERICAN LIBRARY, INC., 1633 BROADWAY, NEW YORK, NEW YORK 10019.

The first chapter of this book appeared in *The Whiskey Guns*, the twenty-first volume in this series.

SIGNET, SIGNET CLASSIC, MENTOR, PLUME, MERIDIAN and NAL BOOKS are published by The New American Library, Inc., 1633 Broadway, New York, New York 10019

First Printing, October, 1983

1 2 3 4 5 6 7 8 9

PRINTED IN THE UNITED STATES OF AMERICA

The Trailsman

Beginnings . . . they bend the tree and they mark the man. Skye Fargo was born when he was eighteen. Terror was his midwife, vengeance his first cry. Killing spawned Skye Fargo, ruthless, cold-blooded murder. Out of the acrid smoke of gunpowder still hanging in the air, he rose, cried out a promise never forgotten.

The Trailsman, they began to call him, all across the West: searcher, scout, hunter, the man who could see where others only looked, his skills for hire but not his soul, the man who lived each day to the fullest, yet trailed each tomorrow. Skye Fargo, the Trailsman, the seeker who could take the wildness of a land and the wanting of a woman and make them his own.

The early 1860s, where the Milk River crossed down from Canada into Blackfoot Indian country, the borderland of northern Montana . . .

1

The big man with the lake-blue eyes grimaced as he uttered a silent curse. He was sorely tempted to turn away. He might well have, had it been a half-dozen range riders able to fend for themselves. He was running late and in no mood for more delays, especially the kind that could be permanent. But there was just the girl and the old man. And the six near-naked bronzed-skin riders. *Damn*, Fargo swore again as he watched. Two of the Indians had raced ahead of the girl and the old man and started to turn to cut them off while the other four came up from the other side.

Fargo swung up onto the glistening Ovaro with the white midsection and black forequarters and hindquarters. He sent the horse into a full gallop, streaking through the widely spaced aspens. The girl, in the lead, short brown hair tossing from side to side, saw the two bucks that had doubled back to cut her off. Fargo watched her rein up sharp, swerve her horse to cut away to the right, and the old man follow her lead. But the maneuver cost precious seconds and the two bucks that had cut her off ran their ponies parallel to her flight, keeping her and the old man boxed in while the other four closed ground.

Fargo drew the heavy Sharps rifle from its saddle case as the Ovaro thundered through the forest. The two bucks were concentrating on the girl and the old man, only becoming aware of his presence when he was almost upon them. He saw the one Indian turn, astonishment flashing in his broad, flat face. Fargo, holding the heavy Sharps by the barrel with both hands, swung with all his strength. Tremendous shoulder muscles propelled the walnut stock that all but knocked the Indian's head from his shoulders as it smashed full into his astonished face. Fargo heard the snap of the man's neck as his face disintegrated in a shower of bone, blood, and tissue. The second Indian tried to duck away from the onrushing horseman but Fargo switched his grip on the rifle to use the heavy stock as a battering ram. He rammed it straight forward, the blow catching the Indian in the solar plexus as he tried to lean sideways on his pony. The buck's mouth came open as a rush of air exploded from inside him and his face twisted in deadly agony as he fell from the horse, hands still clutched to his midsection, his own horse stomping his body crazily with its hooves.

Fargo saw the other four bucks ride up, and one, a scrawny figure, begin to leap from his pony at the girl. But she twisted away, hung half over the side of her horse as the Indian missed his leap. He slid from the horse's rump and hit the ground. Fargo saw the girl rear her horse and bring his forefeet stamping down on the figure on the ground. One thudding hoof crashed down on the Indian's backbone and the man's scream was made of shattering pain.

"Bastards. Rotten, lousy bastards," Fargo heard the girl scream with the sob in her voice, too caught up in her own fury to see the brave moving in on her from behind. Fargo swore again as he turned the big rifle in his hands. He hadn't wanted to cause gunshots to sound but there was no other way now. He raised the Sharps, aimed as the Ovaro galloped forward. The red man's arm was upraised, a short-handled tomahawk in his hand. He started to bring it down on the back of the girl's skull when Fargo fired. The heavy slug tore through the buck's back, in between his shoulder blades, and he stiffened, his arm still raised high, as though suddenly frozen in place. Fargo saw the girl turn to see the Indian behind her, and there was fright and surprise in a snub-nosed, not unpretty face. The Indian, still standing frozen, but his back now a running sheet of red, toppled backward over the pony's rump, stiff in sudden death.

Fargo didn't wait to see him hit the ground as he spun the Ovaro in a tight circle. The third buck raced at him, only a few feet away, and out of the corner of his eye, Fargo saw the old man on the ground, trying to fight off the fourth Indian. The girl spurred her horse on to go to the old man's assistance and Fargo's attention returned to the Indian hurtling at him. He saw the arrow already on the short bowstring and he flattened himself across the pinto's withers as the Indian let the shaft fly. Fargo felt the feathers brush the top of his hat as the arrow cleaved the air. He looked up to see the Indian, bow drawn again, about to send another arrow at him, this one too close to miss. Fargo let himself roll from the far side of the saddle, making himself stay loose as he hurtled from the racing horse. Even so, he felt the jar in every bone in his body as he hit the ground and a cobwebbed curtain came over his eyes. He lay still, gasped in pain as he turned, shook his head. The cobwebs parted just enough for him to see the near-naked figure leap from the Indian pony, come at him with something glistening in one hand. Fargo rolled again and once more the pain in his body made him gasp. He shook his head again. The cobwebs came apart with agonizing slowness. Through eyes still blurred, he saw the figure leap at him, the glistening object taking shape as a long-bladed hunting knife.

Fargo let himself go backward as the red man came down on him and got his shoulder away just in time to avoid the knife that plunged into the ground. He brought one powerful arm up in a backhanded blow, felt it crash against the side of the Indian's head, and the man fell away. The jar of the blow broke away the last of the cobwebs and Fargo saw the Indian, a short but wiry figure, regain his balance and come in with the knife slashing out in a short, flat arc. Fargo sucked breath in and the blade grazed his stomach. Off balance at the end of his vicious swipe, the Indian tried to pull back but Fargo's looping left crashed into the side of his face. The short, wiry figure pitched forward, landed on its knees, tried to spin around. But Fargo had the big Colt .45 out of its holster, smashed the barrel into the man's temple. The Indian uttered a short gasp of pain as he fell sideways, tried to bring his knife arm around again, but his movements were now slowed. Fargo crashed the heavy Colt down on the man's skull with all his strength and felt the splintering collapse of bone. The red man's breath became a sputtering sound as he collapsed on his face, quivered for a moment, twitched again, and lay still.

Fargo's eyes darted upward to see the girl cursing and screaming as she clung to the back of the last Indian, who tried to smash his tomahawk down on the old man beneath him. As Fargo got to his feet he saw the girl pull the Indian's bear-greased hair with both hands. The buck let out a roar of pain, flung himself from the old man and the girl went sprawling onto the ground. He started to bring his tomahawk up when he glimpsed the big, black-haired man racing at him with the Colt in his hand. He turned, flung the weapon, and Fargo twisted sideways as he dropped. The tomahawk whistled past his head as Fargo hit the ground. When he looked up, the Indian was vaulting onto his pony, digging heels into the horse's ribs. Fargo raised the Colt as the pony streaked away, the buck clinging to its back. Fargo took aim but his finger didn't tighten on the trigger, and slowly he lowered the six-gun. Once again, he wanted to avoid the sound of gunshots, and he rose to his feet as the Indian disappeared into the trees.

He saw the girl beside the old man, helping him to sit up as she pressed a kerchief against a bleeding cut on his temple. A deep bruise also discolored the old man's neck where a tomahawk had just missed ending his life. Fargo walked toward the pair, saw the old man's face, strained but gray-blue eyes clear under a shock of white hair that made his weathered face seem to be fashioned out of parchment. Fargo's eyes went to the girl and saw that his first, fleeting impression had been right. She was pretty, her snub nose covered with a half-dozen freckles, brown eyes in a square, slightly pugnacious face framed by the short, brown hair. She let the old man hold the kerchief to his temple and got to her feet, her eyes moving up and down the big man's powerful frame.

"We owe you, mister," she said, her face set, grave. "Thanks doesn't say much."

"It'll do," Fargo said. He let his eyes move over her, saw nice, square shoulders, a figure not over five-five, very round breasts that pressed smoothly into a tan shirt open at the neck. Round, full hips gave her a slightly chunky appearance but a rip in her riding skirt revealed a nicely turned calf.

"You have a name, mister?" she asked.

"Fargo . . . Skye Fargo," the big man answered.

"You the one they call the Trailsman?" the old man asked as he pulled himself to his feet, a tall, narrow figure but still unbent despite his years. Fargo nodded and the old man's gray-blue eyes stayed on him as he held the kerchief to his temple. "We were more than lucky," the man said.

Fargo's glance went to the girl and back to the old man and he made no effort to keep the exasperation from his voice. "What the hell were you two doing riding alone out in this country?" he asked.

"We weren't alone," the girl answered, and Fargo saw the effort it took to keep her lips from trembling.

"Robin's brother and her cousin were with us," the old man said. "They caught the first four arrows."

Fargo watched the girl, saw her eyes look away as she managed to hold back tears. "The bastards. The murderin', stinkin' bastards," she muttered, and the sob was in her voice again.

"What happened?" Fargo asked the old man. "They jump you by surprise?"

The old man frowned. "No, we saw them and we moved away. They turned and came after us hell-

14

bent for leather," he said. "We were just getting near the Milk River and looking for a spot to cross. We didn't want trouble. They could see that. But they come after us with only one thing on their minds and that was to kill every damn one of us." He shook his head and Fargo saw the wonderment in his old eyes. "I've been chased by the Blackfoot before. Usually if you hightail it they'll break off after a spell. You show 'em you don't want trouble and they'll just chase you far enough to make sure. Not always, of course, but most times. But these, they were out to see that nobody got away." He shook his head again and frowned up at the big man before him. "They'd have done it except for you. Like Robin said, thanks is a mighty small word."

"Robin?" Fargo asked.

"Robin Daley," the girl said.

"I'm Amos Baker," the old man said.

"So you had two young men with you. I'm still asking, what were you doing out here?" Fargo said.

"We'd picked up stakes. We were heading out to try and find a place we could settle down on," the girl answered. "My brother Todd and his cousin Scobie, they helped Amos and me try to work a small piece of land. But we couldn't make anything of it and we decided to quit and find someplace else."

"The boys were cowhands. They'd no turn for growing things," Amos Baker cut in. "And Robin here couldn't make it go by herself. So they all decided to move on."

"And that's all done with now," Fargo heard the girl say, the half sob and bitterness curled in her voice. "All gone in a few seconds. All finished by a

15

few stinkin' arrows." Fargo watched the old man put his arm around her as she buried her face into his thin, narrow chest. "I want to go back and give them a decent burial, Amos," she murmured. "A decent burial. I've got to do that."

"Going back could get you buried, too," Fargo said, not ungently.

"I don't care," Robin Daley flared, straightening up, and Fargo saw the pugnaciousness come into her face, adding its own kind of attractiveness to her. "I'm not leaving Todd and Scobie for the coyotes and wolverines," she said.

Fargo shrugged. Logic and common sense held no candle to love and grief, and he met the old man's eyes, saw agreement there. "You don't have to come along, Fargo. You've done enough," Amos Baker said. "I'll go with her." Fargo saw the old man's mouth thin out as he met the message in the lake-blue eyes. "I'm not much for dyin' alone," Amos Baker said. "Can't think of a better person to do it with than Robin."

Fargo looked past the two figures, his eyes scanning the trees, mostly aspen and black walnut. Nothing moved, but the one buck had fled alive. Chances were better than even that he had friends not too far away. "I was riding to the Milk River anyway," he said.

Robin stepped to him, her brown eyes peering up at him. "I won't be forgetting this," she said.

"I've a feeling I won't be either," Fargo said grimly.

Amos Baker took the kerchief from his temple. The cut had stopped bleeding. "I still can't figure why those Blackfoot were so all out to murder us," the old man said. "Unless maybe they're taking to the warpath in a big way."

16

Fargo turned and strode to the nearest lifeless figure. He knelt down, peered at the almost naked form, let his eyes linger on the Indian's moccasins. He rose, walked to where the next still form lay facedown on the grass. The man wore a wrist gauntlet and Fargo lifted the limp wrist, frowned as he studied the design cut into the buckskin gauntlet, a squared pattern of markings. He dropped the Indian's arm, took three quick, long strides to the third figure, and peered down at the man's moccasins where a similar squared design had been cut. He saw Amos and Robin move toward him as he turned from the Indian.

"What is it?" Robin Daley asked.

"No Blackfoot," Fargo said. "These are Cree."

"Cree?" Amos echoed, his weathered face breaking into astonishment. "The Cree up in Canada, across the border," he said.

"Not these five," Fargo said.

"What the hell are the Cree doing down here?" Amos asked.

"That's a good question, Amos," Fargo said. "You can be sure of one thing. They're not here because they lost their way."

2

Fargo let his eyes slowly move over the five slain Indians. The Cree were dead but they spoke just the same, Fargo thought. By their very presence they spoke even as their message lay cloaked in death's shroud. Amos Baker's voice echoed his thoughts. "Why?" Fargo heard the old man ask, the single word a Pandora's box of questions.

Fargo shrugged as he lifted his eyes to the parchment-skin face. "Maybe they just came down to raid," he offered.

Amos Baker made a half-snorting sound. "They come a long way from home just for raiding," he commented.

Fargo's wry smile held appreciation in it. Amos Baker was sharp, the comment astute. "You're right," he agreed. "But I'll ride with that till I've something more."

"Guess there's nothing else to do," the old man conceded. Fargo heard Robin's voice cut in, turned to see her brown eyes deep and grave.

"You think there's something more?" she questioned.

The big, black-haired man shrugged again. "I don't know and I don't much want to think about that. I'd rather hope not," he said. "Let's go do what needs doing." He swung onto the pinto and waited as Amos pulled himself onto his horse.

"Back this way." Amos Baker gestured and Robin Daley brought her horse alongside him as he moved forward. Fargo swung the glistening Ovaro behind her and the old man, but his eyes peered past the two figures as they rode. He swept the foliage ahead, noting the turn of the leaves, the lay-back of low-hanging branches, the stillness, and the sounds, watching, listening, reading the terrain the way most men read a book. When Amos halted he spurred the Ovaro forward and spied a still form on the ground a dozen yards on.

"You stay here," Fargo said to Robin as he rode on with Amos beside him.

"Scobie," Amos noted grimly. Reaching the body, Fargo dismounted, broke off a low branch, and used it as a pick to dig up the ground. Amos worked beside him, and with their bare hands and pieces of branches they dug a simple, shallow, crude grave, marked it with a cross fashioned of branches and tied together with a length of lariat. Robin came up then, knelt down, and Fargo watched her determinedly hold back the tears that pushed at her.

"Should be maybe another hundred yards on," he heard Amos say, and he nodded, following on foot as Amos led the way. The old man was some fifty yards short when they came upon the silent form, three arrows sticking up from it. Amos worked beside him again and when they were finished, Robin came forward and this time the sobs refused to be denied. Fargo walked a dozen yards on to let her be alone with her grief. He had sat down on a piece of log when she came up to him, her eyes rubbed dry but the pain still in her face.

"Thanks, again, for everything," she said.

Fargo nodded at her, let his eyes take in the pugnacious prettiness of her, made more so by grief and the anger that gave her a grim vibrancy. "What now?" he asked as Amos came up.

"We go on," she said, and he caught the half sob still in her voice.

"Just wandering?" Fargo frowned.

"We were on our way to cross the Milk River. We'll try again," Robin said.

"Just you and Amos?" Fargo pressed.

"Yes," she said. "We've gone through plenty, Amos and I. We can do it."

Fargo let his thoughts show in his eyes and saw the pugnaciousness come into her face. "What are you thinking?" she tossed at him.

"Sort of like the deaf leading the blind," Fargo answered.

"That's a rotten thing to say," she flared. "You saved us but that doesn't give you any right for saying a thing like that, Mr. Fargo."

Amos's voice cut in, his tone reprimanding yet gentle. "Robin, girl, face up to it. The man's not far from the truth," Fargo heard him say.

Robin's eyes turned on him, indignation and pain in them, and her freckles seemed to grow deeper as her face colored. "How can you say that, after all we've done together?" she accused.

Amos's smile held gentle understanding. "They were other years and other places for us, Robin," he answered. "We'd be dead now except for this man, and we had Todd and Scobie with us. How far are the two of us going to get?"

Fargo watched as Robin spun away to stride into the trees, halt a dozen yards away, her back to them. "She's a feisty one but she's easily hurt inside," Amos said softly to the big man beside him. "I guess I ought to feel good that she still looks up to me so."

"You should," Fargo agreed.

"When her folks died I practically raised her and her brother, but that was over ten years ago. She forgets. Ten years is nothing when you're twenty. It's everything when you're seventy," Amos Baker said, and there was sadness in his voice.

Fargo's smile was wry. "The young never think that way," he said. "And maybe it's right that they don't."

"Maybe," the old man agreed as he ran a hand through his still-thick white hair. "But she'll have to face the truth, just as I have to face it."

Fargo saw Robin turn, start to walk back toward them. She halted in front of him, her lips tight but her brown eyes unwavering, her very round breasts still smooth mounds under her tan shirt. "I'd no cause to snap at you so after what you've done," she said. It was a statement, not an apology, Fargo noted and smiled inwardly.

"Mount up," he said. "Crossing the Milk may take more doing than I'd figured."

"Dammit, Fargo, stop saying things sideways," Robin snapped.

"Meaning what?" Fargo asked mildly, quietly amused at her acuity.

"You're saying you could make it easy if you were on your own," she threw back, brown eyes flashing dark fire. He let his smile answer. "Well, then you just go on your own. I wouldn't be asking anything more of you," she flung back, pride coating every word.

"No, you wouldn't be asking but you're here and that's enough," Fargo said.

"What's that mean?" she frowned.

"I can't be turning my back now any more than I did before," Fargo said and smiled to soften the words. "Now stop being so damn bristly and fall in behind me, single file," he said and set off. He glanced back to see Robin follow, Amos falling in behind her, a white thatch bobbing along. Fargo rode slowly, carefully, making his way through the aspen till he reined to a halt and slid to the ground, motioned for the others to do the same. He took the pinto by the cheek strap and led the horse forward, pausing often, his nostrils flaring at each halt, ears straining, drawing sound and scent into himself. The trees grew thicker, the aspen giving way to alders and Rocky Mountain maple, a sure sign they were nearing the river. Suddenly he stopped, his nostrils twitching at the suddenly strong scent of bear grease. He backed the pinto, led the horse into a dense thicket, and Robin and Amos followed. Fargo put one finger to his lips and gave Robin the pinto's reins to hold as he stepped from the thicket, dropped to a crouching lope, and moved forward. He followed his nose and picked up the scent of the bear grease, an unmistakable odor he had come to know all too well.

Another dozen yards forward he dropped to one knee as he saw the three horsemen. The river was still hidden beyond the thick foliage but it was close, he took note, as his nose picked up the smell of mud banks and the musky odor of musk grass. The three horsemen came closer, moving slowly, and he felt the frown dig into his brow. Two Cree and one taller, finer-featured Blackfoot. Silent as a rock, Fargo watched as one Cree turned toward the river and moved out of sight. The other Cree continued on and the Blackfoot slowly doubled back the way they'd come. They were not out scouting, not simply riding. They were patrolling. Fargo frowned. He stayed motionless until the Indians were all out of sight and then pushed himself backward, turned, and stayed in the crouch as he made his way back to the thicket. He took the reins from Robin, refused her questioning eyes as he motioned for silence, and led the way back at least a hundred yards before halting.

"Two Crees and one Blackfoot," he said as the others sat down in front of him. "Patrolling along the side of the river."

"Patrolling?" Amos echoed, his gray-blue eyes widening in surprise.

"That's right, patrolling," Fargo repeated. "And I'll wager there are others doing the same."

"What the hell for?" Amos said. "Unless they're looking for us. One did get away. Maybe he told them we'd try crossing."

"Not likely. He'd have no way to figure that. Most folks would be running the other way," Fargo said.

"Strange, the whole thing is strange, the Cree down here with the Blackfoot," Amos muttered.

"What now?" Robin asked.

"It'll be dark soon. We'll try to cross by night," Fargo said. Robin leaned back as he tied the horses under a heavy-branched maple. She was watching him as he returned, silent musings in her eyes.

"I'm going to take myself a nap," Amos said. "I'll be needing the extra energy come dark."

He rose, tall and straight, walked past the maple where the horses were hidden, and sank down out of sight in the high brush. Fargo's eyes returned to the girl, saw her eyes narrowed as she watched him. He let his gaze move slowly over the twin mounds under the tan shirt, still absolutely smooth in their fullness. "Damn few have done more than get to look," she snapped out.

"You proud of that?" Fargo asked.

"It's the way I wanted it," she said.

"Why? You afraid?" he queried.

"I am not," she bristled. "I just never met a man worth being with for more than a half hour."

"Maybe they felt the same," Fargo remarked.

"Maybe," she returned, her chin lifted, her face full of defensiveness. "Tonight, you figure to sneak across the river?" she asked.

"Yep," Fargo answered.

"It'll never work, not with three horses." She sniffed disdainfully. "They'll hear us or see us."

"It'll be tricky but it can be done, with a little luck," Fargo said.

She shook her head in disagreement. "Only one way to do it," she said. "Get as close to the river as we can and then ride hell for leather. We can be across by the time they get themselves together."

"Like hell," Fargo said, his tone milder than his words.

"I tell you it's the only way," Robin insisted.

"It's the only way to get dead quick," Fargo said. "We do it my way."

"What's wrong with my way?" Robin pressed.

"It stinks," he told her. "You don't want to do it my way? Don't come along. Do your own thing later."

"Damn, Fargo, you could at least discuss it," Robin protested.

"I just did," Fargo said, laying back with hands behind his head, and closing his eyes. He felt her simmering; she took awhile but he heard her finally move and settle herself against a tree. He catnapped as the remainder of the day slipped away, woke as the air changed character and became the cool of night. His eyes found Robin nearby, against the tree, her knees drawn up, a lost, despondent figure. She saw his eyes on her and pushed the lostness from her face, letting a glower take its place. Fargo stretched as Amos appeared, pushed himself to his feet.

"Got some jerky in my bag if you're hungry," Amos said.

"Later, thanks," Fargo said. "If I'm able to be hungry then," he added with grim humor.

Amos found a stretch of log and eased himself down onto it. "You never did tell what you're doing up in this country, Fargo?" he said.

"On my way to see a man, name's Roy Patterson," Fargo said. "His spread's the other side of the Milk."

"Roy Patterson? He's got a name in this part of the country," Amos said.

"What kind of a name?" Fargo asked.

"He's known as a hard-driving man, the kind of man who gets what he wants," Amos said.

"And doesn't care how?" Fargo asked.

Amos Baker frowned in thought, adding a few more lines to his parchment face. "No, can't say I've heard that about him. He's hard and demanding, I'm told, but he's fair. Knew a few men who rode for Roy Patterson. They never liked him but they respected him. He's a cattleman," Amos said.

"He's hired me to take a herd of his top stock across the border into Canada, up into Saskatchewan Province," Fargo said. "I'll get the details when I get to his place. *If* I get to his place," Fargo added, correcting himself. He glanced up at the sky to see the moon starting to climb high and he rose. "Time to move," he said.

Robin's voice cut through the night, petulant and stubborn. "I'm not going," she said.

Fargo watched Amos turn to her in astonishment. "What'd you say, Robin?" the old man asked.

"I said I'm not going," she repeated, more snappishly this time.

"What in tarnation's got into you, girl?" Amos frowned.

"He knows," Robin said, gesturing with a toss of her head to the big man.

Amos turned questioning eyes; Fargo's face had hardened. "She always this damn dumb?" he rasped.

Robin rose, stepped closer. "I'm not following anyone who won't explain or discuss anything," she said angrily. "You could at least give reasons."

"I could do a lot of things I don't do. You trust me or you don't," Fargo returned.

"Robin, the man's the best there is. We're more than lucky to be with him," Amos interjected.

"You taking to siding with strangers, Amos?" she snapped at the old man as she whirled and stamped away.

Fargo heard Amos, his voice lowered, apologetic. "She's upset. She never took to being given orders, anyway," Amos said.

Fargo took six long strides and reached Robin as she stared into the night, her back to him. His hand closed around her arm, pulled her around to face him, did so hard enough for her short brown hair to swing from one side to the other. "You lost your brother and your cousin. You hurt bad inside. You're full of hurting and hating and you have to hit back. I know that and that's the only goddamn

26

reason I'm taking time with you, you hear me?" he bit out, his face hard. She blinked but made no reply. "You want to ride hell for leather across the river?" Fargo pushed at her. "You know the mud holes in that bank? You know how the bank drops off? You know the current and the depth of the river at this point? You know any damn thing about the Milk?" He saw her swallow, blink again. "But you want to ride hell for leather in the dark. Well, you go ahead, honey. Just don't expect me to come get you," Fargo said, spun on his heel, and strode away. He heard her voice, suddenly small.

"Fargo . . ." she called. He paused, let her catch up to him. "I'm sorry," she said. Fargo's eyes stayed ice blue.

"I heard that before," he said.

"Can't say you won't hear it again," Robin said. "I follow what I feel." She could be pugnacious and plaintive at the same time, he took note, a combination with its own brand of appeal.

"Get your horse," he said. "Lead him on foot." He turned from her and brought the Ovaro from the maple tree, started through the darkness, moving slowly, easing the horse past low-hanging branches. He had gone some hundred yards toward the river when he halted to let the others catch up. Robin moved to stand beside him, her eyes questioning.

"We strip down here," he said.

"We what?" she frowned.

"Undress. Get clothes off," Fargo snapped and watched her eyes cloud, her little pug nose seem to quiver. He began to peel his shirt from powerful shoulders.

"You're joking," Robin said, and his eyes, cold

27

ice, bored into her. "You're not joking," she corrected.

He pulled his shirt free, began to fold it. "You going to get out of those clothes?"

"You'd just love that, wouldn't you?"

"I might, only I won't have time to enjoy it." He started to unbuckle his gunbelt.

"Why? What in hell makes this necessary?" Robin shot back.

"Keep your damn voice down," Fargo hissed. "You know, you're really becoming a pain in the ass, honey?"

"I still say why?"

"The Indian uses his nose as much as his eyes, especially at night. Do the same myself. He'll pick up the smell of wet clothes instantly. Wet cotton, wet wool, wet pants, they give off their own odor pretty damn quick." He paused, watched her lips stay pursed. "Now you going to get those clothes off on your own or do you want help?" he hissed, swung the gunbelt free. He half smiled as she turned, marched around to the other side of her horse, and began to undress. "Roll your clothes in your saddlebag and they'll stay dry," Fargo said as he began to unbutton his pants and strip down. Amos was in underwear when Fargo finished putting his own clothes into his saddlebag, the old man suddenly looking frail in his near nakedness, arms thin, body narrow. He saw Robin, behind her horse, her eyes moving over his magnificently muscled body and he kept his smile inside as he turned, started to lead the pinto forward. Amos swung in behind him, he saw, Robin bringing up last, staying close to her horse.

Fargo brought his attention to the dark forest ahead as the leaves trailed across his skin. He paused every few feet to listen and sniff the air. The scent of the river came to him, suddenly strong in the night air. They were close and he pushed forward through the thickness of a box elder, halted as the Milk River suddenly appeared in front of him. He took in a thick growth of arrowheads along the near bank, sniffed the slightly musky odor, and motioned for the others to move closer. Amos dropped to one knee beside him and he watched Robin come up, her eyes staring straight ahead as though she were completely alone. He kept the smile inside himself. Pale pink bloomers couldn't hide a slight tummy, a fleshy sexiness in its outward curve. The breasts were indeed full, pushing out with round proudness, so smooth when under the blouse because the tiny nipples were flat, almost inverted in the center of surprisingly large, pink areolas. Robin Daley's figure echoed her face, a spunky, pert body, exciting in its full-fleshed, rounded vitality.

"From here you move slow. No hurrying unless something goes wrong," Fargo whispered. He started forward, motioned instantly with his hand as he halted. The half-silhouetted figure came further into his vision, moving slowly on horseback along the riverbank. Fargo watched the Indian halt, scan up along the bank, turn, let his eyes move back along the foliage. The red man's eyes traveled past the box elder where the three figures crouched in breathless silence, moved on to peer down along the riverbank. He turned, guided his horse to the very edge of the river. He was not idly taking in the night, Fargo muttered inwardly. He was patrolling and Fargo felt the frown touch his brow. He told Amos and Robin to stay in place with a quick, sharp glance, handed the old man the pinto's reins, and moved forward through the trees.

He moved on silent, cat-paw steps, crouched low, his lake-blue eyes riveted on the Indian. He'd left the calf holster strapped to his leg, the throwing knife inside the leather sheath, and now his hand moved down, drew out the double-edged, needle-point blade, often called an Arkansas toothpick. Silence was everything. Fargo grimaced. There were others not far away, he was certain. The Indian's back was to him, the range close enough for the knife to do its work. But it wasn't enough. The man could crash to the ground, making a loud enough sound to alert others. Or the blade could strike just a fraction off, just enough to let him emit a gargling cry. No, he had to get closer, Fargo knew, much closer. He crept forward, bent almost in two, each step set down with careful pressure, and he felt the tiny beads of perspiration form on his forehead.

The Indian was only a few feet from him now, close enough for him to see the flat face with the broad, flattened cheekbones. Cree, Fargo murmured to himself, unmistakably Cree. He halted, stayed in the crouch as he raised his arm, the double-edged blade in his hand. He drew his arm back and, with a short, whipping motion, sent the knife hurtling through the air. As the blade cleaved the dark, the Cree turned, his eyes widening as he saw the near-naked, white figure. But before he could open his mouth to shout, the blade struck, crashed through his throat, penetrating all the way, halting only when the hilt hit the bottom of his chin.

The Cree grasped at the object spilling his life away, his hands clawing helplessly at the blade for an instant as his eyes seemed to almost fall from their sockets, and then he toppled from the saddle. But Fargo was there to catch him, prevent him from crashing to the ground, and he eased the limp form down. He pulled the blade out of the man's throat, stepped back as the small torrent of red gushed forth. Crouching, he listened, ears straining, but there was only the night forest sounds and the soft lap of the river against the shore. He rose, waved a hand, and Amos came forward first, Robin behind him, still staying close to her horse. Fargo took the pinto from Amos and moved toward the river. As the others watched, he eased the pinto sideways into the water, letting the horse almost slide in at an angle so as to make the least possible amount of noise. He saw Amos begin to follow suit and he stayed close to the pinto, began to drift more than swim, one hand at the horse's head, fingers curled around the concha and brow band. Once into the water, he eased the pinto in a half circle to head for the opposite bank.

In midstream, his eyes swept the far bank, saw nothing move and headed for a pair of low-hanging sandbar willows. As he neared them, his feet touched bottom and he made his way up on the bank, moved under the low-hanging willow branches. He pulled a towel from his saddlebag, dried himself some as he waited for the others to reach him. He was half dressed as Robin emerged from the river, looking beautifully shiny and wet, her skin shimmering even in the dark. She stepped behind her horse at once to dry and dress. When she and Amos finished, Fargo motioned to them, led the way on and out along the back side of the willows. He didn't mount the pinto till they were at least a hundred yards from the river, didn't speak till they had ridden another fifty yards. "We'll ride some before bedding down for the night," he said.

"What happens when they find the one you did in?" Robin asked.

"They'll search around and see that three horses crossed over but that'll be it. They'll figure us too far gone to chase over the countryside," Fargo told her.

"Come morning?" Amos put in.

"Not then, either," Fargo said, and felt the frown come to his brow. "They're up to something. They're patrolling the river, at that point, at least. Damned if I can figure why. Or what the Cree are doing down here and part of it."

"No good will come of it, you can be sure of that," Amos said, and Fargo nodded agreement. He turned up a slope, rode into a long stand of cottonwoods, and slowed the pinto to a walk. He halted when he came to a small, clear space amid the trees.

"This will do us for the night," he said, and watched Robin slide from her horse, weariness in her face. Her skin was still damp, and the blouse clung to her round breasts, their smoothness unbroken even against the clinging fabric. "We'll make the Patterson place tomorrow," Fargo said as he put down his bedroll and pulled off clothes. He was stretched out in the bedroll when he heard Robin's voice, the question sliding at him from where she lay under a blanket.

"What happens then?" she asked. She tried to sound merely curious but the anxiety was there in her voice, an undertone she couldn't hide.

"Can't see cutting you loose there, if that's what you're asking," Fargo said.

"I wasn't asking that," she snapped too quickly, and Fargo smiled into the dark.

"Get some sleep," he said, turned on his side, the big Colt .45 at his fingertips. He closed his eyes, still wondering why the Cree were here with the Blackfoot, his thoughts echoing Amos's remark. There'd be no good come of it.

3

The first sign of the Patterson ranch was a pair of stone gates set out by themselves, no fence leading from them. They looked as though they'd been misplaced, but they marked a road, and Fargo trotted between the gates and followed down the path. It had taken the better part of the day to reach the spread and he had watched Robin grow more tense with each passing hour.

"You always get yourself so worked up?" he had asked mildly as he saw the tight set of her jaw.

She flashed him a sharp glance. "Got a bad feeling," she said.

"I think you're afraid you might have to take favors and you don't like that," he commented.

Her little nose went up into the air. "That's part of it," she conceded. "But the rest stays. I've a bad feeling."

"Too much pride can twist you up," he remarked, and her face told him he'd struck a tender place.

"I suppose you think that's what's stopping me from jumping into your bedroll," she snapped, eyes flashing darkly.

"You sure pull things out of a clear sky." Fargo laughed.

"No clear sky. I saw the way you looked at me last night."

"I saw the way you looked at me," he answered mildly, and her freckles seemed to deepen as she colored.

"It wasn't the same thing."

"Hell it wasn't." He smiled. Her eyes flashed angrily as she pulled her horse around and rode back to stay beside Amos. Fargo rode on and reached the first of four large corrals, fences neatly painted, in good condition. The stock inside was made up of white-faced Herefords, all in top shape, he noted. He passed a half-dozen hands at work, saw they were all young men. He glanced back to see Amos and Robin hanging back, almost halted, and he rode up to the large, U-shaped, low-roofed house, stone on the bottom, good cedar shingles above. It murmured rather than shouted wealth.

He dismounted and turned to see the girl come from the house, walk toward him, and he found himself unable not to stare. Striking was the word that flashed in his mind, striking more than beautiful. The full, jet-black hair, worn shoulder length, could have belonged to a Cheyenne maiden, but not the alabaster skin, the absolutely eggshell white made to seem more so by the frame of onyx hair. He took in a straight, delicate nose, classically formed lips, the lower one slightly fuller than the upper. But it was the eyes that held him, blue he'd only seen once before, on a sled dog, a Siberian husky, very round, pale, pale blue, yet electric, ice-floe blue, and yet in their depths, a strange burning, eyes that were a physical contradiction. She was tall, he noted, perhaps five-ten. A pale, blue shirt buttoned high tried hard to match her eyes but failed entirely. It stretched tight across well-rounded, full breasts, womanly breasts, and his gaze followed down to a good waistline tucked in enough and opening into hips, perhaps a trifle wide, that curved into long legs under a dark blue riding skirt. She carried a quirt stuck in the belt of her skirt. Her brows lifted, twin, thin arches that gave her a faintly disdainful air.

"Fargo?" she asked. He nodded. "I'm Eden Patterson."

"Eden?" he echoed. "That's a mighty nice name."

Her tiny smile was a quick flash. "How nice of you to say." She managed to make the remark sound as though she couldn't care less. Her voice, like the eyes, was a contradiction, the tone velvet soft, the delivery wrapped in icicles. "We expected you two days ago," she said, a hint of reprimand in her tone.

Fargo let his eyes meet hers with matching coolness. "Don't recall any timetable," he commented.

She took the faint admonishment with her almost perfectly formed lips flashing a thin smile. She let her eyes move up and down his hard-muscled, magnificently balanced physique, and the ice-floe orbs hid whatever she was thinking. He saw her glance go past him to where Robin and Amos had halted a dozen yards away. "They with you?"

"For now," Fargo said. "They were going to lose their scalps when I came onto them."

Eden Patterson's eyes returned to him. "My father's inside. Please follow me," she said, making the invitation sound like a command. He let his eyes linger on a nice, round bottom and hips that swayed just enough as he walked behind her into the house. She led him through a foyer with stone flooring, into a vast living room, to which heavy wood and leather pieces managed to lend

36

some warmth. He knew he failed to keep the surprise out of his eyes as he he saw the man in the wheelchair, a large-framed man, the chair hardly able to contain his bulk. He had the girl's face, the same black hair, straight nose, round eyes but not as pale.

"This is Skye Fargo, Father."

Roy Patterson's eyes took on animation. "Well, now, this is good news. You made it. I was getting worried." The man's deep, resonant voice fitted his presence, commanding even in the wheelchair. "I suppose you're surprised to see me in this chair."

"Wasn't expecting it," Fargo conceded.

"Neither was I two weeks ago," the man boomed out, sudden anger in his voice. "Goddamn horse tripped and I landed on a rock, split my hip. The doc said it might heal if I stay at least six months in this damned contraption." Fargo felt the frustration cascade from the man. Roy Patterson's heavy hands gripped the arms of the wheelchair as though he wanted to tear them away.

"Tough luck," Fargo said.

Roy Patterson turned to his daughter. "Get the man a drink, Eden. You forgetting your manners?" he bellowed.

Eden glanced at Fargo, unruffled, cool, completely poised.

"Bourbon," Fargo said, and she nodded, moved across the room to a finely carved wall cabinet.

"Sit down, Fargo. We've some talking to do," Roy Patterson boomed in a voice used to commanding and to being obeyed. Fargo eased himself into a leather chair almost opposite the man, watched Eden return with his bourbon, her breasts swaying ever so slightly in unison as she moved with graceful, almost gliding steps. He nodded to

37

her as he took the glass, lifted it and drew in a deep swallow.

"Good bourbon," he remarked.

"Only the best," Roy Patterson said.

"Does this mean you'll be letting your foreman drive the herd?" Fargo asked as Eden perched on the wide arm of a heavy chair. Her skirt opened to reveal a beautifully long calf.

"Hell, no. Don't have a foreman. Never had one. I've always been my own foreman," Roy Patterson shot back, and he saw the question form in the big man's eyes. "Eden, here, will drive the herd," Roy Patterson said. Fargo saw Eden catch the surprise in the quick glance he tossed at her. "Eden knows everything there is to know about cattle and cattle driving. Hell, she was raised out there beside me. She's better than any hand I ever had. She's tops and she's hard-driving. Hell, her daddy taught her how to be that."

Roy Patterson paused to throw out a booming laugh but Fargo caught the harsh sound inside it, the bitter anger of a powerful man stripped of his power. Roy Patterson paused to draw in a deep breath and Fargo let his eyes go to the girl. He saw Eden Patterson meet his narrowed glance. They were like twin masks, those pale ice eyes, revealing nothing, he saw and returned his glance to the big man in the wheelchair.

"You get her through, Fargo. She'll see to the rest, take my word on that. She's Roy Patterson's daughter," the man said as though he could transfer all he knew and all he was to his daughter by sheer will.

Fargo took another deep pull of the bourbon. "Let's hear the rest," he said, his voice flat.

"You'll break trail into Canada, to Big Moose. Ever been in the Saskatchewan country, Fargo?"

"Not that far into it," Fargo said. "But a sign's a sign, no matter where you read it."

"That's true enough," Patterson said. "Now, I've got to tell you, there may be trouble along the drive."

"You know about the Cree?" Fargo asked.

Roy Patterson's brows drew together. "The Cree?"

"They've come down across the border, tied in with the Blackfoot. Something's in the wind."

"No, the Cree have come down because Saskatchewan is having problems," Eden interjected. "Too little rainfall, the soil dried out, the game dying off. That's why the Cree have come down."

"And that's why we're getting the price we are for our herd," her father added.

"There's something more. They're not just down here looking for game or raiding," Fargo said.

"Nonsense," Eden answered. "That's exactly what they're down here for."

"And if the Cree give you any trouble, I assure you that Eden and my hands can take care of a few red savages," her father said. Fargo said nothing as he grimaced inwardly at Roy Patterson's arrogant stupidity and heard Eden's low, velvet voice answer his thoughts.

"Fargo doesn't agree with that," she said, condescension in her voice. Fargo allowed her acuity a small smile of approval.

"No matter. He'll find out," Roy Patterson said. "The real trouble will be coming from a man named McMurtree, Tom McMurtree. I figure he'll try to take the herd."

"Why?" Fargo questioned.

"McMurtree and I had a business deal once. He

didn't hold up his end of it and I got rid of him. He's been out to get back at me ever since. This would be the best chance he's ever had," Roy Patterson explained, used his big arms to lift himself as he shifted in the wheelchair, the effort making him grimace angrily.

"How many men are you sending with the herd?" Fargo asked.

"Eight. That's all I have to send and it's enough. With you and Eden it makes ten, plenty to take care of McMurtree."

"What makes you so sure?" Fargo queried.

"I've my own channels. I was told he hired six cheap gunslingers. With his own men, that won't make more than ten or twelve, and McMurtree's basically a coward. He'll have no taste for hanging in when there's rough going."

Fargo wondered whether the man's driving arrogance caused him to underestimate others. Besides, he'd seen more than enough cowards swallow their feelings when the rewards were worth it. He finished his bourbon and got to his feet, his tall, powerful frame unfolding, seeming to stretch almost to the low ceiling of the room. He saw Roy Patterson studying him.

"It's more than you bargained for, isn't it?" the man commented.

"Never saw a job that wasn't," Fargo said. "But I'll admit you've thrown in a few new ones."

"Such as my leading the drive?" Eden Patterson cut in, the pale ice eyes narrowing ever so slightly.

Fargo half shrugged and made no comment.

"You do the job, you get a bonus, Fargo," Roy Patterson said quickly.

"Never turn down good money." Fargo smiled

and saw Eden stand up, tall and regal, a kind of Amazon-like air to her full figure.

"I'll show you around," she said, and walked toward the door. Fargo nodded to Patterson as he followed her outside. He spotted Robin and Amos, dismounted, talking to two cowhands against one of the corrals. Eden Patterson halted, half spun to him, her eyes frigid. "You don't think I can do the job," she said tightly.

"I don't think you know what you might be up against," Fargo said mildly.

"I can handle the herd, the men, and anything else that comes along," Eden replied, looking very beautiful, her icy anger giving her a new cold fire.

Fargo shrugged again. "One thing we'd best get straight. Once we hit the trail, I call all the shots," he said.

"I'm in charge of this drive, Fargo," Eden snapped.

"You're in charge of the cows, honey."

"How dare you. You're working for me."

"On the trail, you're listening to me."

Her lips tightened. "We'll discuss this further." Her eyes went to Robin and Amos. "You're friends are waiting to say good-bye."

"They're not saying good-bye. They're coming along," he said calmly.

The pale blue eyes stared at him. "What did you say?" Eden Patterson emphasized each word slowly.

"I said they're coming along till they can find a safe place to cut loose," he answered. "It's not here and it's not out there with the Cree and the Blackfoot up to something."

"They go on their way alone," Eden said.

"No way. It'd be handing them a death warrant," Fargo told her.

"Look here, you're being paid to lead the trail,

not to do good deeds"—Eden's eyes flicked to Robin—"or enjoy your rewards in your bedroll."

Fargo half smiled. "Well, now, that last makes me wonder," he said.

"Wonder what?"

"If maybe there's some plain old-fashioned female jealousy behind all that bitchiness," he said. "It's a good sign if it's so. Shows you're not all ice."

"You can stop wondering. I want your full attention on your job, nothing else. No distractions for you or any of the men," Eden said. "They go their way here and now."

"They go, I go," Fargo said matter-of-factly.

"Damn, Fargo, you've got your nerve giving orders." She frowned.

"No orders, just the way it is," he said calmly.

The pale blue eyes glared for a moment. "I'll introduce you to the men," she said, abruptly switching signals. It was a kind of concession by default, he recognized, decided not to press her for more. She walked with brisk, purposeful strides, and he caught up to her as she waved to some hands working in one of the corrals. The men came at once, five of them, climbed through the fence rails, respect for Eden in their manner. Perhaps a kind of caution, Fargo mused silently. They were mostly young, the world not yet marking their faces with hard lines. Except for one, a narrow-shouldered cowpoke with small eyes and a tight line of sourness in the set of his mouth.

"This is Fargo. You were all told about his coming to lead the trail for us," Eden said.

"Glad to meet you. I'm Tom Craft," the nearest hand said, and Fargo returned the greeting with a nod.

"You're the one they call the Trailsman," another said. "Heard about you back in Kansas."

"Don't believe everything you've heard." Fargo smiled. Eden introduced each of the men but Fargo didn't bother remembering names. He'd learn them on the trail. But the sour-mouthed man's name stayed with him, a rhythm to it . . . Al Allgood.

"You can meet Howie, Bert, and Rob tomorrow," Eden said. "They're helping birth a calf in one of the barns. I presume we'll be moving out tomorrow?"

"Don't see why not," Fargo said.

"Anything special you want to tell us?" one of the men asked.

"Can't think of anything. You know your jobs. I know mine. That gives us a good start on anything," Fargo said. The men turned away and began to go back to the corrals and Fargo slid words at the young woman beside him. "They know about this McMurtree feller?"

"They know there's bad feelings between my father and him," Eden Patterson answered.

"They know McMurtree's out to try for the herd?" Fargo pressed.

She took a moment before answering. "No," she said, her voice flat. She turned the pale blue orbs on him. "Daddy saw no reason to alarm them," she said.

Fargo's smile was thin. "Daddy saw no reason to be honest," he corrected. "Some of them might have pulled out."

The pale blue eyes grew frostier. "You always give a nasty twist to things?"

"You always sugar-coat things?" he returned. Eden halted as they drew near where Amos and Robin waited, barely outlined now in the fast-gathering dusk. "Come over, I'll introduce you," Fargo said to her.

"Tomorrow will be more than soon enough," Eden said, icy disdain in her round eyes. "I'll think overnight about the rest of our discussion. We never finished it," she remarked.

"Yes, we did," Fargo said affably. "You just don't know it."

She spun away from him, the pale eyes flashing a moment of anger, began to walk away. "Eden's still a nice name," he called after her. She didn't glance back. Most women would have stomped off, he thought, but she had too much cool, controlled class for that. She walked away with firm but unhurried steps, hips swaying with quiet provocativeness. He moved on to Robin and Amos. Robin's tension translated itself into pugnaciousness, her pert face set, her little snub nose all but quivering.

"Roy Patterson give you a hard time about us?" she questioned, all defensiveness.

"He didn't. She did," Fargo answered honestly.

"She?" Robin frowned.

"Eden Patterson. She's taking the herd through. Her pa's got himself a broken hip."

"That settles it. I'm not going," Robin snapped. "I took one look at her and I know her kind."

"What kind is that?" Fargo asked.

"Bitchy. Rotten. Thinks she's better than anybody else."

"Not bad." Fargo smiled. "But you're going along with me."

"No," Robin began, and he cut her off.

"No more out of you," he said with a sudden coolness. "It's settled. You'll be going along."

"Obliged, Fargo," Amos said quietly. "Much obliged."

Robin tossed him a glare. "I told you I had a bad feeling," she muttered.

"Let's find a spot to bed down," Fargo said as he swung onto the pinto and rode off. He slowed when he passed outside the twin gates of the ranch, and Amos and Robin caught up to him as he moved into a stand of tanbark oak, found a small thicket just large enough for two to bed down in it. He gestured to Amos and Robin to take it and rode on, passed almost a hundred yards of sudden rock-strewn soil before he found a little niche for himself between the trees. He bedded down, clad only in underpants on the bedroll, and let his thoughts slowly circle inside his mind. A striking, jet-haired, alabaster-skinned young woman immediately swam through his mind and he wondered how much fire those pale, ice-floe eyes really masked. Just how deep did contradictions go inside her, he wondered. She drifted away in his thoughts, replaced by the Cree, and again he wondered about their presence here, their closeness with the Blackfoot. Trouble, he was damn certain of that. But what and where? When would their savage fury erupt? He was still pondering the question when he heard the footsteps, moving quickly, light yet loud in the still of the woodland. He rose onto one elbow. His hand closed around the Colt, more from force of habit than alarm as he saw Robin come into view. She wore her shirttail out, hanging loose, night ribbons in her hair.

"I was afraid maybe you'd be asleep already," she said, dropping to her knees at the edge of his bedroll. He watched her brown eyes move across his near-naked body, then pull away too quickly. "Just came to say I'm obliged, too. I was wrong back there by not admitting that the way Amos did," Robin said.

"Amos send you?" Fargo asked.

She flared instantly. "Nobody sends me anywhere for anything. I came 'cause I wanted to."

"I'll believe that." Fargo smiled slowly as her eyes flicked to his shorts for another brief instant.

"And I still have a bad feeling about it," she said with a half pout.

Fargo lay back. "Maybe you should have," he said, and told her about Tom McMurtree. "Between him and the Cree, maybe I haven't done you a favor by bringing you along on this drive."

"You saying things sideways again, Fargo? You want us to go on our own? Just say it."

"Jesus, you're so damned touchy," Fargo said. "Now, why in hell would I want that all of a sudden?"

She gave a half shrug. "Eden Patterson is a very beautiful woman," Robin said. "Maybe you like it better alone with her."

"If I want that, I'll have it."

Robin's pert nose turned upward. "You're awfully sure of yourself, aren't you?" She sniffed.

"Just about some things," he said. "Such as the reason you really came here."

"I told you why I came," she bristled.

He sat up, reached a big hand out and curled it around the back of her neck as he pressed his mouth on her lips. "I heard you. It was a half-truth. This is the other half," he said.

"No," she murmured. He pressed his mouth down. She didn't respond. She didn't pull away either. His hand moved down from the nape of her neck, slow pressure down along her back as he let his tongue reach out, push through her lips, savored the taste of her, warm, sweet, wet. He felt the soft rush of breath from her opened lips as he let his tongue dance along the top of her lower lip. "No," she murmured, but the word was almost inaudible and her hands tightened against his shoulders.

He let his hand drop lower, come around and up under the loose shirt, rest against the soft skin of her ribs. "Oh, oh ..." she murmured. He let his hand move up under the loose shirttail until his thumb touched the underside of one soft breast. "No, oh, God," Robin gasped out, squirmed, pulled her lips from his, and in her eyes he saw the dark turbulence. "No, Amos is too near," she breathed.

"Maybe," he conceded, let his thumb move from the underside of her breast, pulled his hand out from under the shirt. She quivered, a deep sigh escaping her lips. "Next time you'll have to plan better," he remarked.

"I didn't *plan* anything," she flared at once.

He laughed. "Maybe your head wasn't in on it but the rest of you was," he said. She tried to wrap indignation around herself as she rose, but he saw her eyes flash over his body once more. "Next time," he murmured, and she turned, strode away, and the dark closed around her. He smiled, lay back, and let sleep come to him. The night stayed still and he slept soundly until the morning sun filtered through the trees in little streaks and dots. He washed with water from his canteen, brushed and saddled the pinto and led the horse to where he'd left Robin and Amos. Only Robin greeted him, one hand brushing her short brown hair. She answered the question in his glance.

"Amos went on ahead to talk to her," she said.

"To Eden Patterson?" Fargo frowned.

"Amos is a proud man. He'll be offering to earn

his way. He'll be offering for both of us," Robin said.

"He should've checked with me, first," Fargo said unhappily.

"Why?"

"I could've saved him time and pride. It's the wrong move at the wrong time." He swung onto the pinto. "Meet me at the ranch," he said, and cantered away. He was almost at the ranch when Robin caught up to him, slowed at his side as he drew near to the main house. He saw Amos there, Eden Patterson facing him, looking almost as tall in a black shirt and black riding britches, a white sash tied around her waist. Contrasts, he grunted, stark contrasts. It fitted her. The quirt was at her side, held by the sash. It was part of her attire, he decided. He moved closer, caught Amos's words.

"No pay, of course. I'll ride herd, round up strays, take care of the horses, whatever you want," he said. "But I can help out, earn our way along, Miss Patterson."

Fargo watched Eden Patterson's striking face. It stayed the icy mask he had expected it would, the pale blue eyes piercingly disdainful. "I'll think about it. Perhaps there might be some boots that need cleaning," she said. Fargo saw the moment of hurt touch the parchment face as Amos turned away from the icy eyes that continued to stab at him.

"*Bitch!*" Robin hissed beside Fargo. "I'll tell her what to do with her boots."

Fargo's hand pulled back on her horse's cheek strap as she started to send the animal forward. "You'll stay right here and keep your mouth shut," he growled. Robin glared at him and pulled her horse around, rode to where Amos was climbing into the saddle. Fargo trotted the Ovaro toward

48

the long, straight-backed woman in the black shirt and black riding britches. He halted before her. Eden Patterson's eyes were beautifully pale twin masks as she met his angry stare. "You've got a lot to learn, honey," he said.

"About what?" she returned.

"About people," Fargo snapped.

"I know all I need to know about people," she tossed back.

"You don't know shit about handling people." Her eyes narrowed. "The man came to you in good faith. He offered you all he had to offer. He didn't deserve that kind of bitchy, slap-in-the-face answer." Her eyes stayed narrowed. "Or maybe you don't want to understand. It's easier that way."

He saw the ice-floe eyes flicker, but her lips tightened at once. "I'm here to see that things are done the way they should be. I don't have to understand anyone for that," she answered.

"Hell, you don't," Fargo snorted. "You want to get the best out of people you better understand what makes them tick."

Her eyes stayed coldly disdainful. "I don't care what makes them tick so long as they do tick," she said.

He grunted wryly, fastened her with a sharp glance. "You do your thinking last night about my calling the shots when we hit the trail?" he asked.

"You'll call the shots," she said through lips that hardly moved. "Daddy's decision, not mine," she added tersely, and he half smiled at how she was quick to disassociate herself from the decision. "I talked to him and he said he'd hired you because you were the best and he'd have to go all the way with you."

"Good," Fargo said. "You ready to move out?"

"Yes. I'll tell the hands to start them rolling."

Fargo watched her ride off, stiff-backed, and he went to where Amos and Robin waited, she with the anger still in the pugnacious set of her face, he with tired eyes. "Hell, maybe she's right," Amos commented to Fargo. "Maybe shining boots is all I'm good for anymore."

"Don't say that, Amos," Robin cried out, anger and empathy in her voice. "She's just a rotten-tongued bitch."

"You picked the wrong time, Amos," Fargo said. "She's lost a few rounds with me and she took it out on you. You work with me on this drive, Amos. I'm thinking I'll be needing help."

Amos nodded and Fargo saw the surge of restored pride flow through the parchment face. Robin moved alongside Fargo, her voice low and tight. "You making excuses for her," she hissed.

"No, and see to it I don't have to make any for you," he snapped back, spurred the pinto forward to watch the steers begin to move from the corrals. It was a hell of a big herd for the handful of cowpokes, he muttered to himself. But the men were good, he noted, working smoothly and efficiently to pull the mass of cattle into a single, manageable unit. Eden rode back and forth and Fargo decided Roy Patterson hadn't exaggerated about her. She was quick, barked out orders with precision. She seemed to be able to sense where a half-dozen steers were about to break out and got a cowhand to cover the spot at once, helped out if it was needed, using her mount with the least amount of unnecessary motion. He heard Amos's voice echo his thoughts as the herd moved past.

"She's damn good," the old man murmured. "Got to hand that to her." Fargo nodded, saw

Robin's face stay tight as she refused comment. He moved the pinto on past the herd, which began to spread itself sideways but stayed under control. He passed Eden as he moved on in front of the herd, saw that her face seemed to soften, the ice go from it, as she worked the herd, a strikingly attractive figure as she leaned back and forth in the saddle, her long body graceful, supple, her breasts dipping and lifting in unison. He rode on, stayed a hundred yards in front of the herd, and rode slowly, casually.

The beginning was easy. They mostly always were, he reminded himself, in easy-riding, easy-herding flat country. When they started up into the hills, he moved on further in front of the herd, let his eyes quickly sweep the terrain ahead. Hilly but flat enough for the cattle, he noted, and turned back to the herd, paused beside Amos and Robin. "I'm going to scout on ahead. You stay here," he said to Amos. "Watch, take in everything. Eden started out good. I want to know if she can keep it up."

"I won't miss much, you can count on that," Amos said.

"I'll ride along with you," Robin cut in.

Fargo hesitated, considered, decided against it. He intended a quick, initial survey of the land. He'd be moving fast, looking only for specific signs this time. Company would slow him, he decided. "Some other time," he told her.

"I'm not going to ride along here looking useless," Robin protested. "You told Amos to watch what goes on. I want something to do."

"You watch Amos," Fargo ordered, and sent the Ovaro into a fast canter. His attention returned to the terrain at once. The rolling hills were heavily

51

wooded, not the best place to drive cattle. He rode up on a high mound, surveyed a passage between a stand of balsam firs and a slope of red cedar. Somewhere to the north the Milk River would be crossing down from Canada into the northern Montana territory. Heavy woodland lay between him and the river now. The first good spot to cross a herd was where he had slipped over with Robin and Amos. And where the Cree and Blackfoot patrolled, he grunted. Perhaps they had moved on, he speculated, and rejected the thought with a frown. His sixth sense told him to discard the thought, a gut feeling that had nothing to do with ordinary common sense. The Cree had come down to the river, left their homeland. They wouldn't be pulling out so quickly. They had plans, they and the Blackfoot.

His eyes moved across the land, peering, seeking, straining, searching for anything that might indicate a place to turn the herd north toward the Milk. But the woodland stayed thick and unbroken to the north, and he thought about the man McMurtree. He could easily be in that heavy woodland, Fargo mused, watching, pacing the movement of the herd, biding his time. Fargo turned the Ovaro in a tight circle. There'd be time to check on McMurtree later. He had seen enough for the moment and he started to double back the way he'd come when he reined up sharply, his lake-blue eyes narrowed at once. A distant stretch of low branches moved in a line. Possibly an elk, he murmured to himself. Or a lone horseman. Fargo took the pinto into a heavy stand of trees, worked his way downward; not a single branch moved as he guided the horse delicately, carefully, threading his way through the trees. He drew a slow circle that brought him back up behind the line of branches that continued to move as they were brushed past.

He moved forward and picked up the sound, no elk or moose but a horse's hooves. He quickened his pace, guided the pinto through the trees, and came in sight of the horse. He felt his breath draw in sharply as he saw the slender figure on the horse, short brown hair bobbing from side to side. "Goddamn," he hissed as he spurred the pinto forward in a sudden burst of speed. She turned in the saddle as he rode up to her, surprise flooding her face. "What the hell are you doing out here?" Fargo rasped.

Robin bristled defensively at once. "Just riding. Any law against that?"

"Yes, goddammit, my law. I told you to stay with the herd."

"And I told you I wasn't going to ride along looking useless," Robin returned.

He stared at her in angry disbelief. "You plumb crazy? You were lucky once. You trying for a second chance at losing your scalp?"

"I was keeping my eyes and ears open." Robin glowered.

"Sure you were. That's why I had so much trouble coming up on you." Fargo saw her face grow red. "I ought to send you packing for a dumb stunt like this," he said.

"Go ahead," she said defiantly, her pert face lifting upward.

"I would but Amos would go with you and he doesn't deserve to get himself killed because of you." Fargo spoke harshly and saw his words hit hard as her lips grew tight. Her mouth opened to snap back a reply as he heard the sound in the

53

brush. His hand shot out, clapped itself over her mouth as he yanked her to the ground with him. He lay half atop her warm softness, his hand still over her mouth. He saw the fright in her eyes as she tried to wriggle free. He pressed harder against her. "Be still," he hissed as he listened to the sound in the brush grow nearer. She lay quiet as she picked up the sound, too, the fright staying in her eyes. Fargo stayed motionless, his ears attuned to the sounds. He read their message as only he could. A horse, one single horse, moving slowly but not tentatively. No pauses to look and listen, the movement steady, unbroken. No Indian, he thought as he caught the faint click of rein chains. He watched the trees move as the horse drew close and felt Robin's fingers pulling at his hand over her mouth.

He took his hand away but stayed half atop her and drew the big Colt .45 from its holster, rested his hand lightly on one round, full breast. The horse pushed through a half-dozen branches to come into sight, and Fargo's brow furrowed as he saw the man collapsed in the saddle, his head fallen forward onto the horse's withers. Five arrows pushed up from the man's back like so many colorful porcupine quills. Fargo pushed himself to his feet, holstered the gun, and reached the horse in six long strides. The animal halted as he pulled the figure from the saddle, laid the man on the ground. He heard Robin come up beside him as he bent low over the man.

"He's still alive, but not by much," Fargo said. "Give me his canteen."

Robin unwound the canteen from the saddle. Fargo opened it, sprinkled some of the water over the man's face, a middle-aged face, ordinary enough, with an unkempt beard that was more gray than brown. He wet the man's lips with the water, sprinkled more on his face. The man's eyelids fluttered, came open, tried to focus. Fargo lifted the man halfway to a sitting position, let more air fill the man's lungs. His hand felt the sticky wetness that drenched the arrow-filled back. The man's eyes slowly focused, stared, and his lips moved. But only a hoarse hiss came from them.

"Easy, now," Fargo said, and the man's lips moved again, opened wider, and once more only the hoarse wheeze came from him. Fargo lifted his head and shoulders a little higher. The man's mouth moved again, and the sound came as though squeezed through a funnel, hoarse, strained, vocal cords barely able to respond. The single word came from the man's dry lips.

"Warn . . ." he gasped, and slumped back against Fargo at once. He shuddered as his eyes half closed.

"Warn about what?" Fargo asked. He shook the form gently, shook again, and the man's eyes struggled open again. Fargo watched the man move his lips once more, the effort consuming, pain-filled.

"Warn them . . . the Cree . . . warn . . ." he gasped, and his hoarse, wheezing breath trailed the words into nothingness. Fargo felt the shudder pass through the man's body and then the sudden limpness, that special kind of limpness that bespoke only one thing. Fargo let the man slip from his arms to the ground, stared down at the silent figure with his lips pulled back grimly. He rose to his feet, used the water left in the canteen to wash the blood from his hand. As Robin looked on with eyes filled with apprehension, he rifled through the man's saddlebag and found a receipt for a secondhand bridle.

"His name's Jim Oddle," Fargo said, and then, with grimness in his voice: "He was crossing the Milk when they caught him."

"What makes you think that?" Robin questioned.

"His horse. It's wet up to the brisket and ribs. Saddle skirt and fender's all wet, too," Fargo said. His eyes went down to the arrow-riddled form. "Warn them?" he repeated. "Warn who?" His glance went to Robin and she shrugged helplessly. Fargo's eyes lifted, traveled in a circle, scanning the thick woodland. "Stay with the horses," he told Robin. "I've no time or tools to do it proper but I'll do the best I can." He stalked off, pulled down young, thick-leafed branches till he had over a dozen. He dragged the man to one side and fashioned a small pallet out of the branches, hung the man's hat and gunbelt on a length of branch driven into the ground, and turned away. He mounted the pinto and handed Robin the reins of the other horse. "We'll take him back. An extra mount always comes in handy," he said.

He rode slowly, in silence, the man's last, gasped words hanging like an unseen shroud. Warn them, he repeated again. What had he meant? Warn who? Perhaps a wagon train somewhere near? Fargo held on to the possibility as he rode into more open land and his eyes swept back and forth, seeking signs of a wagon train. But he saw nothing yet; it was a big country. A wagon train could be traveling almost anywhere beyond his vision. But had the man meant a wagon train, Fargo pondered. Or something else? His thoughts continued to circle. Had the man come onto something? Was that what he wanted to warn others about? He pulled his lips back in disgust. Speculation was worthless, offering nothing of substance. But the man's words stayed, clinging, a silent riddle. He rode in silence until the herd came into view. Eden had called a rest break, he saw, and his glance flicked to Robin.

"You damn well better remember what I said back there about you riding out alone."

She made no reply but her face wore more contriteness than anger.

He reached the herd, dismounted. Eden came over at once, her eyes taking in the extra horse. He told her quickly about the man he had found and his last, gasped words. Eden listened, her lips pursed.

"A general warning," she said crisply. "But of course you already knew the Cree were here."

"He meant more than that," Fargo said.

"Conjecture on your part," Eden said, dismissal in her tone.

"Knowing inside," Fargo said.

"No matter. Your job is getting the herd through, nothing else," Eden said coldly, turned, and strode away. Fargo saw Amos move nearer, the old man's eyes apologetic as they glanced first at Robin and then back.

"She took off afore I could stop her, Fargo," he said.

"Figured that," the big man replied. Robin walked away, her little pug nose turned skyward.

"The Patterson girl runs a tight ship, Fargo," Amos reported. "She keeps her eye on everything that goes on. She hasn't let up once."

Fargo watched Eden remount, and the men began to do the same. Howie, the young blond boy, Tom Craft, Rob Boyson, the others he'd only briefly met, and the last to remount, Al Allgood. The man's sourness hadn't seemed to have changed any as his small eyes lingered on Eden for a moment,

Fargo noticed. Eden turned her horse to Al Allgood. "You'll ride tail now, Al," she said. Fargo saw the man hesitate, seem to be about to say something, but Eden's very direct, cool eyes changed his mind. He swung onto his horse, the sour lines of his mouth a little deeper.

Under Eden's direction, the herd began to move forward again. Fargo eyed the sun in the sky. There was more than enough of the afternoon left for a proper scouting expedition. No general survey, this time. Now he'd seek signs, details, the messages trees and earth would tell him, the words of the land, the language of the Trailsman. He nodded to Amos and moved away, paused alongside Eden.

"Keep the herd moving through that open land straight ahead, between the slopes," he said, and she allowed a faint nod. He cantered away, turned after a hundred yards, and moved up the slope through the trees. The country was heavily wooded but broke out in brush-covered rock ledges at unexpected places, he noted. He'd not ridden more than five minutes when he heard the hoofbeats coming up behind him. He turned, one hand on the Colt in its holster at once. He saw the flash of the white sash against the black shirt and skirt, then halted and let Eden come up to him.

"The herd's moving quietly. I thought I'd ride along with you for a spell," she said, making the statement sound like a command.

"I ride alone," he said.

"Not in this case. I like to see things for myself."

"I don't give sight-seeing tours," he growled.

"And I want to see what I'm paying for." Her tone was imperious.

Fargo's eyes narrowed. The answer was true enough, as far as it went. But there was more.

Curiosity was part of it. Conceit another. Distrust the last part. He felt the sudden frown touch his brow as a puff of breeze brought his nostrils drawing in the scent.

"What the hell is that?" he barked. She frowned in question. "Perfume," he said. "I didn't catch it back there with the herd."

"Cologne," she corrected. "Gardenia. I like to keep fresh even on the trail."

"Get it off," Fargo rasped.

Eden's pale blue eyes grew a shade darker. "You have a nerve. I certainly will not. What I wear is none of your concern."

"When you're riding trail with me it is. All I can smell is you. Get it off."

"Well, you'll just have to live with it. Most men find it attractive."

Fargo touched the pinto with his reins and the horse moved forward. Eden swung alongside him, too pleased with what she took as a minor victory to pay attention to his chiseled handsomeness. He turned the pinto to the soft, splashing sound and reached the small, fast-running mountain stream that spilled into a freshwater pond at one side and continued on out the other. He halted, fastened lake-blue eyes on Eden.

"You going to wash that damn stuff off or do I do it for you?"

"You wouldn't dare."

"I'd dare and you'll get a lot wetter if I do it," he said.

Her hand went to the quirt stuck inside the white sash. "I know how to use this," she warned.

"I'm sure you do. Then you can get your little ass back to the herd. You're not riding with me. I'd like it better that way, anyway."

"I'll ride wherever I please, Fargo. You don't give me orders," she flung back. She turned her head to emphasize the haughty dismissal of her tone. It was but the briefest instant but it was all he needed. His arm shot out like an uncoiled spring, a sweeping motion, connected with her just below the shoulders. She sailed out of the saddle and hit the pond with flailing arms and legs, the loud splash punctuated by a short scream, surprise and anger in it.

Fargo vaulted from the pinto into the pond, landed beside her as she came up sputtering. He yanked the quirt from the sash before she could begin to reach for it, flung it onto the dry ground.

"You bastard," she exclaimed, her pale blue eyes sending out flashes of fire as she swung at him. He parried the blow, caught her arm and spun her around to take hold of her, one big hand closing around the back of her neck. He plunged her into the water, immersed her, held her there just long enough to make her gasp for breath, then pulled her up. He rubbed his hands over her face in a washing motion, rubbed behind her ears, down along her neck, and his arm felt the swell of her breasts. He plunged her into the water again and repeated the process. The alabaster skin was creamy soft to the touch and his hands caressed as much as they washed. When she regained her breath and started to fight, he spun her away and stepped back, was out of the pond in two long strides.

"*Bastard!*" he heard her scream. "You stinking bastard." Eden pushed her way from the pond, fury in her face. "I ought to fire you. Maybe I will," she shouted.

"Just tell me soon as you make up your mind," Fargo said calmly.

"Bastard. Just who do you think you are?" she yelled back.

"Somebody who wants to stay alive." He let his lips edge a smile. "You're not all ice," he said, and his eyes moved over her, lingered at the beautiful twin curves made by the black shirt as it clung to her breasts. She noticed his observing eyes, spun on her heel, and rummaged in her saddlebag to come out with a blue shirt and a towel. She strode behind a row of tall, bright orange mullein that successfully hid her from view. She reappeared in a few minutes wearing the blue shirt and holding the wet one in her hand.

"I won't be forgetting this, Fargo," she said, her fury now controlled.

"Me neither." He smiled affably. "Your skin is damn nice to the touch."

"You won't be touching it again," she retorted as she retrieved the quirt.

His broad smile stayed. "Maybe not," he said. "But don't take any bets." He swung onto the pinto and rode away, chose a path drenched by the afternoon sun, and let the heat dry his pants. Eden caught up to him as he halted, his eyes sweeping the ground where a thicket of sweetclover covered the ground under the shade of a half-dozen common elder trees with their pale yellow flowers.

"What is it?" she asked as she came up.

His eyes met hers, his face unsmiling. "I might be resting. Or I might have seen something. You tell me," he said. She was the kind who only took lessons that dug hard into her, he'd decided. He watched her eyes move quickly over the spot, go to the trees, peer down again, the alabaster brow furrowing in tiny lines.

"There's nothing here," she concluded.

"Nothing to you. Plenty to me," Fargo remarked casually. Her frown stayed and he gestured with one hand. "Over there, the sweetclover," he said. "It's just springing up again. It was flattened. Somebody slept there under the elder trees." He swung from the pinto and knelt down at the spot as surprise flooded her lovely face. "Indian," he said flatly.

"How in heaven can you know that?" Eden queried.

"A white man would almost certainly be wearing boots. When he got up, the boot marks would bruise the sweetclover. These are only flattened, not bruised," Fargo said, and rose, pulled himself onto the pinto, and moved forward. Eden followed, came alongside him, rode in silence, and he smiled inwardly. She broke the silence after a few minutes.

"Just one Indian?" she asked, and he nodded. "What would he be doing out there alone?"

"Scouting," Fargo said.

Her lips compressed. "What are you thinking?"

"Something's up. The Cree and the Blackfoot. That poor bastard wanted us to warn somebody specific."

"You're supposing again," she said. "In any case, it's not your concern. Leading the herd through is your job." She paused and the severity slid into her voice again. "You hear me, Fargo?"

"I hear you," he said blandly. His face remained impassive as her eyes narrowed at him. He moved forward, his eyes roving back and forth as he rode, missing nothing, and suddenly the trees thinned and he rode onto a stretch of brush-covered rock that rose sharply on both sides. His eyes swept the ridges, the rock ledges that ran along the stretch just over their heads, and he suddenly halted. He saw Eden watch as his nostrils flared and he drew in a deep pull of air. He moved forward and felt the Ovaro go into short, prancing steps, and he tightened gently on the reins, a soothing motion.

"Easy, easy," he heard Eden say as her mount grew nervous. She ran one hand along the horse's neck to calm it. "What's the matter, boy? Easy ..." she murmured. Fargo moved slowly along as he drew the heavy Sharps rifle from its saddle case and saw Eden's frown. "What is it?" she asked.

He made no answer as his eyes continued to sweep the rock ledges just above them, moving from one side to the other. He rested the butt plate of the stock on one leg, his finger on the trigger of the Sharps as it pointed straight upward. The sudden roar came at the same instant as the tawny shape flashed into sight, leaping down from one ledge to the one just above their heads. The cougar's long, muscled form was in sight for but that brief instant but Fargo knew its next appearance would take the form of a diving leap. He swung the big Sharps around, fired at the ledge just as the mountain lion's head came into view. The shot sent pieces of rock scattering into the air but he heard the cougar's claws on the rock as it spun, darted away out of sight.

"That'll keep him away," Fargo said as he lowered the rifle. "A cougar will avoid trouble unless he's starving." He turned to Eden, saw the pale blue eyes rounder than usual, her lips slightly parted.

"How'd you know he was up there?" she asked.

"Smelled him," Fargo said blandly. "Same as the horses did." His eyes bored into her with the sharpness he kept from his voice and she looked away. The object lesson had hit home. She'd remember, not that she was about to admit it. He kept the smile to himself as he moved the Ovaro forward. She rode quietly beside him, watching, listening in subdued silence. He pointed out an old, worn piece of deer hide. "Blackfoot. Maybe a month old," he said. Later, a row of young twigs broken off in a line drew more of his attention and his eyes went from the broken twigs to the ground and back again as he followed the path. "Indian ponies. Unshod," he grunted. "Four riders, two, maybe three hours ago." He turned from the line of broken twigs and threaded through the woodlands to come out on a grassy slope that led down to a flattened path. "We can circle the herd around to here," he said. "This will take us on a spell."

"North, to the river?" Eden asked.

"No. We stay this side of the Milk until I find out more."

"About the Cree?" she questioned. He nodded and caught the disapproval in her face. The light suddenly turned gray as the sun slipped down behind the mountains.

"Let's head back," he said, turning the pinto.

"No sign of McMurtree," Eden said, words that were as much question as comment.

"Not yet," Fargo said. "I figure he's waiting somewhere, got a rider out watching, maybe." Eden became silent again and it was only in the last few minutes of dusk, as they came in sight of the herd, that she spoke.

"All right, you wanted to teach me a lesson and you did it," she said, her voice tight. He glanced at her face, beautifully ordered once again. "You're more than good, much more. It's a special talent."

He made a wry sound. "You make nice words

sound like nothing. That's a special talent, too," he said.

"I'll skip saying thank you," she snapped tartly.

"Me, too," he returned.

She halted as they reached the herd, her eyes on the big, black-haired man beside her. "What happened doesn't change my ideas any. You forget about warnings, the Cree, everything but getting my herd to Big Moose," Eden said.

"I'll try," Fargo said laconically, and drew a flash of cold fire from her eyes. She spurred her horse on and he watched her ride away, back straight, the full, womanly breasts lifting in unison as she posted to the cowhands at the herd. She called a halt for the night and set to helping the men settle the herd down. He heard her give out shifts for the night watch and dismounted to see Amos coming toward him.

"See anything?" Amos asked.

"Not much. No sign of a wagon train or anybody else to warn," Fargo said. Someone got a small fire started and Robin appeared with an iron skillet in hand. After Eden, she somehow seemed like a little girl, a fresh-faced brat but nonetheless pugnaciously attractive.

"Want something to eat?" she asked.

"Not tonight. I'll finish some hardtack I've got," Fargo said.

Her pug nose wrinkled in distaste. "Just passed Eden. You didn't melt her any so far as I could see," Robin remarked with studied offhandedness.

"Wasn't trying to," Fargo said. She gave a grunt of disbelief. "See you in the morning," Fargo said. "I'll bed down away from camp. Old habit of mine. Let's me keep an eye on things."

He led the pinto away and felt Robin's eyes

following him until the night swallowed him up in its black cloak. He found a nest of soft balsam branches a few dozen yards from the camp and up on a high slope of land. He set out his bedroll, lay down, and closed his eyes after he finished the hardtack. He let sleep come at once, set his own inner time clock, and slept for some three hours. The sky was a blanket of silver star drops and he sat up, looked down at the darkened campsite below. The cattle were quiet, a huge, black mass to one side, and he left his bedroll, rose, and swung onto the Ovaro. He rode slowly, a half-moon casting enough light, headed the horse north toward the Milk River.

He rode steadily but cautiously, made good time over land that grew increasingly hilly. He was moving down the far side of a hill that was sparsely covered by common elder when he reined in, his nostrils catching the unmistakable odor of bear grease. He stayed motionless under the branches of a tree as the Indian came into sight, a single rider moving slowly, passing only a few yards from him. The half-moon cast its dim light on the broad, flat face, the hair heavily greased and worn to the shoulders, an elk-hide jacket on the man's shoulders, a flat, shapeless garment. Cree, Fargo spit out silently as the Indian rode on. He moved only when he could no longer see or smell the Cree. He continued down the slope, caught the sight of sandbar willows. The river was near, on the other side of the willows, and he started to move faster, suddenly pulled the pinto in again to dart into the deep shadows of another tree.

A line of Cree came into sight, passed below him, riding parallel to the river, four of them, with a fifth bringing up the rear. Fargo's lips drew in tight. Midnight rides weren't a Cree pastime. They were patrolling, back from the riverbank. There were others still at the bank, he was certain. He stayed on a rock, silent as a lizard, and let the Indians pass by. He peered forward into the willows that stretched to the riverbank and spotted two more riders moving in the other direction. He backed the Ovaro from under the tree and started to retrace his steps back up the hillside. It wasn't time to risk an encounter, not yet. There'd be a better time and place for that. Only one thing was certain in his mind as he rode back toward the campsite. The Cree had swept down from Canada, joined with the Blackfoot, and were patrolling the river. There had to be a special reason; it wasn't just to seek game. He found himself thinking of words gasped out with dying breath. Warn who? Why? What had Jim Oddle known? The questions remained a riddle, their answers stilled by Cree and Blackfoot arrows. For now, Fargo only grunted.

He came into sight of the dark mass that was the herd, caught the low mewing sounds, and made his way to the hill where he'd left his bedroll. It moved, and the Colt was in his hand at once as he leaped from the pinto. He saw the brown hair come into sight, the round, pug-nosed face following. "Goddamn, Robin, you could've been blown away," he muttered, shoving the Colt into his holster.

"I was just waiting," she said, and he saw she wore a very thin, off-white nightdress.

"Just waiting?" he asked.

"And wondering," she said, truculence coming into her face.

"You been out with her?"

"Now why in hell would you think that?"

She shrugged. "You were out riding with her all afternoon. Maybe you did melt her."

He dropped to his knees on the bedroll beside her. "You damn well know better," he growled. "Why don't you stop making excuses for yourself?"

Her arms reached up, circled his neck, drew him down to her mouth and her lips, opened, pressed a soft, wet answer. "All right, no more making excuses," she murmured. He felt the tip of her tongue, tentative, waiting, and he pushed his own tongue forward to meet it. She uttered a tiny gasp and he felt her hands pushing the shirt from his shoulders, fingers moving across his hard-muscled body, pressing, caressing, moving over every part of his torso with an exploring, wondering, testing motion. Her lips clung to his and he reached down, shed gunbelt, trousers, underpants, and then took her nightdress and pulled it up.

She paused, drew her mouth from his, and flung the garment over her head to face him. Her breasts seemed rounder, higher, her body chunkier than when she'd crossed the river all but naked—good shoulders, a short, round rib cage that supported the two full breasts, each tanned, each with dark pink circles centered with tiny pink tips. A slightly convex little belly reached out to full thighs, a little too fleshy, yet it all hung together to give her a throbbing, eager sensuality.

His lips moved down to take one breast, draw it in, soft and warm under his touch. "Ah . . . ah . . . iiieeee," she gasped and fell back onto the bedroll. He went with her, his mouth still holding her breast, and her back arched, pushed upward, pushed the tiny nipple against the roof of his mouth. "Take it . . . all of it . . . oh, please," he heard her murmur, and he felt the tiny pink tip rising, growing firm inside his mouth, felt the excitement in his loins at the sensation. His tongue darted around the little tip and he let his teeth gently bite down on it.

"Aaaah ... ah, God, ah ... wonderful ... oh, wonderful," Robin breathed, words coming in long, breathy gasps. His hands moved, caressed the firm, chunky little body, lingered over the little belly, stroked, played, and Robin's hips began to move, a slow, upward-thrusting little dance. His hand strayed down to the tight little nap, wiry, almost rough, then pushed lower. "Oh, oh, oh ..." she cried, pushing out sounds with softly explosive breaths. His hand moved down again and he felt the moistness of her thighs, her wanting already flowing from her, a soundless, eternal river of welcome.

"Please, please," she murmured, and pushed herself upward against him. "Oh, please, Fargo ... please." He felt her hand move down his body, seeking the pulsating organ that rested against her leg. She found her goal, fingers touching, then closing around its warm strength. "Aaaaah ... oh, God ... oh, my God," she breathed. She pulled, her body quivering, her thighs opening wide, tried to pull him into her but fumbled, lost her hold, screamed in dismay, sought him again, and he moved, let her find him. She cried soft sounds of pleasure. "Please ... pleeeeeease ..."

He moved over her, lowered himself, and her hand came away from his throbbing organ as she lifted herself up to meet him. He slid slowly forward into her warm wetness, enveloping, sweet darkness, and he heard her gasped scream of pleasure. He slid deeper, felt her tightness give for him, heard her half cry, sounds of pleasure and pain all entwined. Her palms flattened against the ground and she pushed upward again; he was all the way into her, resting against the very inner core of her.

"Oh, oh, my God . . . aaaaah . . . ah, God, oh, oh . . . goood . . . good . . . oh, yes," she breathed, as if uttering a litany of pleasure. Her legs came up to wrap around his powerful thighs and her hands encircled his back as she attempted to hold him forever inside her. He felt his own throbbing increase and he moved, slid back, thrust deep. Robin gasped screams as she began to pump with him, sudden, urgent motions. "Aaai . . . iiiee . . . ai . . . ai . . . ai . . . ah . . . ah . . ." she bit out with each push and thrust, and suddenly he felt her fingers curl into fists against his back. He held a moment longer, waited for her, and when he felt her ram upward, her chunky little body shaking, he let his explosion come forth. Her little cries became a sibilant . . . a hushed scream, ecstasy too new, too overwhelming to give full voice. "Oh . . . aaaaah, oh, God, Fargo," she murmured as the whirlpool of pleasure began to slip away. "Oh, oh, good . . . oh," she whispered.

He stayed inside her as she grew limp, fell back as though she were a suddenly deflated balloon. He finally withdrew from her and her hand came to clutch at him instantly, hold his still-pulsating, moist maleness. "Ah, ah, aaaaah," she murmured, a hissed cry of satisfaction as her hand curled tightly around him. She turned to rest against him, fitting into the curve of his muscled chest, her little pug nose pushed against his breastbone. "I knew it'd be wonderful if I waited for the right man," Robin murmured.

"How you'd zero in on me as the right one?" Fargo asked.

70

Her shoulders lifted, rubbed against him as she shrugged. "You just know. Something tells you," she said. She turned, lay on her back, and he let his eyes take in the slightly chunky, throbbing sensuousness of her, a pulsating energy even lying still.

"It comes in so damn many different ways," he murmured.

"What does?" Robin asked.

"Beauty," he said. "Wears a lot of faces, each different, yet everyone its own beauty."

"That a compliment in your sideways way?"

"Guess so," he said, laughed as he bent down, drew one round breast up into his mouth. He felt her body quiver at once, her legs draw up together in an involuntary reaction.

"Ah ... ah, yes ... yes ... oh, Fargo ... again, yes," she said, each word gathering into the other in a rush of desire.

"Never refuse that kind of invitation," he murmured, and brought himself atop her. Robin's arms were around his back at once, pulling him into her. His powerful organ, resting between her thighs, grew erect almost at once, pressed against her flesh, and she gave a tiny scream, closed her legs against it, then drew them open, and he heard the quick gasps of breath she blew against his ear. He answered her wanting and made the night into a starburst of pleasure again. It was better the second time for her as she reached for ecstasy with new eagerness. Her cry was again a thing of hissed sound, again her throbbing crotch was too overwhelmed with pleasure, again the sounds of ecstasy burst from her throat.

She lay beside him afterward, taking longer to regain her breath this time, but finally she nuzzled against his chest, let her finger idly trace little

71

lines across his skin. "What happens after, Fargo?" she murmured.

"After what?" he asked.

"After this job's over?" she said.

"I go on."

"Ever think of settling down?" she asked, and then, seeing the little smile touch his lips, "I was just asking," she snapped defensively.

"No woman ever just asks that question." He laughed.

A half pout touched her face. "I was just asking," she insisted, and knew he knew better. "Well, everybody has to settle down sooner or later," she pushed at him.

"Sooner or later," he agreed with mock solemnness.

"Amos said he'd heard you were searching for some men and you wouldn't be stopping till you found them," she probed.

"He heard right," Fargo said.

"Maybe you'll never find them."

"Found one. I'll find the other two," Fargo said, his voice turning hard at once.

She sat up, studied him for a moment. "Yes, I'm sure you will." Then she pushed herself to her feet and he stood up with her, gathered her in his arms, pressed her against him.

"Still have a bad feeling about the trip?" He smiled.

She nodded vigorously, her short, brown hair bobbing against his chest. "Yes," she said. "Except for this." She pulled back and picked up the nightdress, slipped it over her head, and he watched it fall down to cover her.

"Show's over, curtain down." He laughed.

"For tonight," she returned. She kissed him a

quick kiss and turned, hurried away into the night, and he lay down, drew sleep around himself for the few hours still left of the night. The surprises were far from over for this trip, he knew, and few would be as pleasurable as this one had been.

4

The Ovaro glistened in the morning sun, legs firmly on the flat rock, as Fargo watched the herd slowly pass along below. He had rejoined the camp in time for coffee. Tom Craft had been assigned cook's chores and had sat beside him as he finished the bracing brew.

"The Cree really down here?" Tom Craft had asked. "You expecting trouble from them?"

"Not expecting but I want to be ready," Fargo said calmly.

"Somebody said there was more than a raiding party," the man persisted.

"Don't really know." Fargo decided it wasn't time to sound alarms. It was enough that the men were aware. He finished the coffee and hurried away, shutting off further questions. Then he'd ridden into the high ground, where now, on the flat rock, he watched the herd below. Robin bounced along, face slightly smug and shiny with fresh-scrubbed alertness. His eyes found Eden, saw her watch Robin as she rode by, a faint furrow touching her coolly beautiful face. Eden Patterson could have stepped out of a bandbox, onyx hair shining in the morning sun, a deep pink, crisp shirt making the alabaster skin seem even whiter than it was, the quirt tucked into a wide, brown leather belt.

She remained a contradiction, he thought. She seemed out of place on a cattle drive and yet she outrode the men, moved her horse with absolute control, singled out spots that needed attention, and kept on top of the overall progress of the herd. Fargo caught Amos's eye, waved, and saw the thatch of white hair start to climb toward him. Robin waved, leading the extra horse behind her, and he waved back and watched one of the cowhands, the blond boy, Howie, draw up to ride alongside her for a few minutes. Fargo saw him draw a glance of cold disapproval from Eden, but she said nothing as she herded a steer back in place.

Amos reached him and he turned his attention from the herd below. He gestured to two long high ridges that ran on opposite sides of a valleylike dip, separated by perhaps a quarter mile of thick forest. "You take the left one, Amos, I'll take the other," he said. "It'll save me time and effort. You ride the top of the ridge till it ends, see what's below on either side."

"Am I looking for anything special?" Amos asked.

"McMurtree and his men. But you wave me over if you see anything that spells trouble."

"Fair enough," Amos said, and headed his horse for the distant ridge. Fargo turned to the other, rode upward to find the climb to the ridge harder and longer than he'd estimated, the hillside thick with tree cover and a heavy undergrowth of snow-brush, the tiny blue flowers attached to tough stems that pulled at the pinto's feet. When he reached the top of the ridge, he turned to ride slowly along the path, saw Amos a little farther along on his ridge. The two ridges ran almost parallel to each other on opposite sides of the valley, and Fargo, his eyes searching, kept a distant pace with Amos. He rode along the ridge for most of the day; by sundown nothing exceptional had come into his view. He paused to look across at Amos and saw the hat being waved in the air.

Fargo tossed a quick wave in return to let Amos know he'd seen the signal and pointed the pinto down the tree-covered mountainside. Finally he reached the bottom and began the long climb up to the other ridge. When the pinto finally pulled its way to the top, Amos had dismounted, was squatting down by a dead tree. Fargo followed the old man's gesture down the other side of the ridge and his eyes halted at what Amos had seen, a little clearing with a small blackened spot of earth at the center, all of it almost hidden by tree cover.

"Nice work, Amos. Most men would've missed it," he said, the compliment well earned. "Let's take a closer look." He headed the horse toward the spot, which lay halfway down the mountainside, threaded his way through thick growths of hackaberry, red cedar and balsam. The earth-blackened spot, the remains of a campfire, took shape as he neared it, a few pieces of charred branches still in place. The area was larger than it had appeared from atop the ridge, and he dismounted when he reached it, Amos close at his heels. He took in the stain and the smell of emptied coffee grounds beside the blackened earth. The soil revealed boot marks as well as hoof marks. "This morning," he grunted. "I'd guess a dozen horses."

"McMurtree," Amos said.

Fargo nodded as he climbed back onto his horse. He'd seen all the evidence he needed to see. "They're here, all right," he said.

"They're not the only ones here," Amos remarked. He didn't need to explain further and Fargo uttered a grim snort.

"By this time he's seen that we're staying away from the river so he won't wait any longer for us to swing north," Fargo thought aloud. "That might make him move in sooner."

"Well, we know what he wants and knowing's better than not knowing," Amos said.

Again, Fargo nodded at the grim meaning in Amos's words. They knew what to expect from McMurtree; the man posed no riddle. It was the presence of the Cree that posed a riddle, a riddle whose answer could easily mean savagery.

"Maybe the Patterson girl's right, Fargo," Amos said. "Maybe you should forget about the Cree, just stay clear."

Fargo uttered a short, harsh sound. *"Should* won't have much to do with it," he said. "It'll come down to what I have to do, not what I should do, I'm thinking."

Amos digested the answer slowly, and replied with the authority born of years of hard living. "Things most times come down to that," he said softly, followed the big, black-haired man down the slope. Fargo led the way back to the herd, felt the small frown touch his forehead when the herd wasn't where he'd expected it to be. He turned east, rode slowly, and watched dusk slip over the land like a soft, purple blanket being unrolled. The furrow had dug deeper into his brow when he caught sight of the steers.

They had been halted, a swaying, mewing mass, and he quickened the pinto's pace, Amos on his heels. He passed the forward part of the herd and his quick glance saw most of the men standing off to one side with Robin near, everyone's eyes on the pink-shirted figure. He saw Eden facing Al Allgood, her eyes blazing pale blue fire. Fargo dismounted, saw Al Allgood's mouth had turned down still more at the edges but the man was trying hard to keep reasonableness in his voice.

"I was wrong," the man offered. "I owned up to that already. I just wasn't thinking. I admit it."

Eden's tone turned words into shafts. "That's hardly big of you, seeing as how there's nothing else you can do," she sneered.

"I was riding tail and the steers were all moving along fine. I saw the water and stopped to fresh up some," Allgood said. "I figured to catch up easy enough. I guess I took longer than I expected."

"And fifteen steers left the herd because you weren't where you should've been," Eden snapped. "Fifteen steers that scattered and took us almost three hours to round up."

Allgood's little eyes blinked and he kept his tone contrite. "I didn't think they'd tail off that way. They were moving on fine," he said.

"You didn't think, you didn't expect," Eden spit out icily. "But you knew my orders, didn't you? No dropping off, no stopping, no leaving your post without my permission. You knew that and you knew I wouldn't stand for it. Yet you did it."

"Jesus, I said I was sorry. Nothin' bad happened," Allgood half whined.

"We lost three hours, had to tire out every horse, used up energy and manpower, and we could have lost any or all of those steers. I'd say that's bad enough," she snapped. "You'll be working for half pay the rest of the trip."

Fargo saw the man's face flush. "Half pay? The rest of the trip? Hell, that's not fair. You can't do that," Allgood protested.

"I can do anything I want," Eden flung back. "And it's more than fair, considering what might have happened. Half pay, Allgood. Quarter pay if you pull another boneheaded move."

The man's eyes flicked to the others watching, returned to Eden's stare of icy superiority, and the contriteness vanished from his voice, which erupted with a snarl. "I'm not takin' this from you, lady," he said. "Nobody treats Al Allgood like that." Fargo saw the man start toward Eden, his hands closing into fists. "You need a few lessons, you do," Allgood rasped.

He leaped forward with a sudden rush, hands reaching for her, and Fargo saw Eden yank the quirt from her belt with a kind of lightninglike speed he had to admire. She snapped the short-handled whip and a line of red instantly bubbled diagonally across Allgood's forehead. "Ow, Jesus," Allgood cried out as he half turned away in pain. Fargo saw the man's hand go for his gun, an automatic reaction. He drew the big Colt from his own holster at once, Allgood's gun only half out of its holster. Eden snapped the quirt again, the whip a searing snake, and Allgood's fingers spurted red as the gun fell from his grasp.

Eden stepped forward, struck again with the quirt, the blow lashing across the back of Allgood's neck as he tried to turn away. "Goddamn . . . shit," the man gasped out in pain, half fell, landed on one knee. But Eden moved with quick steps, kicked the gun with one foot, sent it skittering back toward her. She scooped it up with one hand as she waited, the quirt poised to lash out again. Allgood got to his feet, pressing his bleeding fingers against his shirt while his forehead ran red and the back of his neck stained his shirt collar a rusty red.

"Get out," Eden hissed. "You're through. Get out or I'll cut the rest of your face into ribbons."

"Bitch. Goddamn bitch," Allgood flung at her, but Fargo caught a look of respect and cunning creep into the small eyes. "Give me my gun back," the man said.

"What kind of fool do you take me for?" Eden said. "Get your horse and ride. Now, dammit, move."

Allgood swung his small eyes, now tiny pieces of black coal, swept the other men. "You fools can have her," he bit out as he backed to his horse, swung into the saddle. "Goddamn bitch," he shouted as he rode into the gathering darkness. "You'll pay, goddamn you."

Eden dismissed his words with a harsh snort, turned to the other men, her voice controlled, crisp, as if nothing had happened. "We'll be camping here. Calm the steers. Same night shifts as last night," she said. Fargo watched the men hurry off to their tasks, each quiet, tight-faced, yet quick to obey. He moved forward and Eden turned to him, pale blue orbs fastening on his intense, chiseled face, trying to read his thoughts. "Well?" she snapped, defensiveness in the single word.

"You're real good with that quirt," Fargo said calmly. "But you still don't know shit about handling people."

"I handled it right. I had to make a lesson of him for the others."

"Crap," Fargo said, and saw her eyes flare.

"You'd have me let him get by with it?" She frowned angrily.

"Didn't say that. Too little is no good but too much is worse," Fargo returned.

"I want my men disciplined. I insist on that."

"Fairness and common sense, those are part of good discipline. You came down too hard. First, you didn't have to tear him down in front of the others. You should've taken him aside, said your piece, warned him what you'd do if there was a next time. That would've been enough," Fargo told her.

Her eyes stayed coldly stubborn. "That's mollycoddling. I don't tolerate mistakes. A man makes a mistake, he pays for it," she returned.

"Only you're paying for it," Fargo said, and her eyes questioned. "You needed every hand you had. Now you've one less gun to face McMurtree. If you were so all-fired bent to make an example of him, you should've waited till after McMurtree made his move. That would have been common sense, honey."

"Allgood was unreliable. I'm glad I found that out now. No loss. It was necessary to make an example of him. I had to do it," she answered.

"You had to play boss-lady," Fargo remarked.

Eden's lovely lips became a thin line. "Take your weak-sister advice someplace else. I handled it the right way." She whirled and stalked away.

Fargo watched her go, a tiny grunt escaping his lips. His words had reached her but she wasn't the kind to concede anything. There was too much arrogance and icy hardness inside her for concession. Self-doubt was a sign of weakness, an uncertainty she couldn't handle. Amos's words echoed his thoughts.

"She's her father's daughter, all right," Amos said. "Without his years that teaches you how to make being hard mean something good."

"She hasn't said one word to me yet," Robin said. "Damn high-nosed bitch."

"Be glad she hasn't," Fargo said. Amos took Robin's horse with his to unsaddle and tether off to the side.

"Where are you bedding down tonight?" Robin inquired when Amos was out of earshot.

He gestured to the slope. "Up there someplace," he said. He let his eyes hold a smile. "Far enough away."

She bristled instantly. "Damn, you do a lot of assuming. I was just curious. You really have your nerve."

"Guess so," he answered blandly and strolled away from her. Tom Craft prepared a meal of dried beef and beans and it was eaten quickly, almost in total silence, the incident with Allgood still hanging in the air. Finished, Fargo started up the heavily wooded slope, pausing to sweep the herd's dark mass with a practiced eye. The blond wrangler, Howie Crater, had drawn first shift and moved his horse quietly among the steers. The night air stayed quiet, the herd calm, Fargo saw, and he continued on up the slope until he found a spot soft with pine needles.

He bedded down, undressed to his underpants, and his thoughts lingered on onyx hair and alabaster skin, fire and ice, inside and outside contradictions. She had so much to learn and learning would come hard for her. It always did for those who thought they had nothing to learn. He half dozed and figured less than an hour had gone by when he heard the footsteps moving up the slope. He lay with his hands behind his back, listened to the sound of steps searching their way, changing direction, tracking back again, and finally she came into view, the nightdress clinging to the high, round breasts, her face pugnacious as she halted beside him.

"Dammit, you could've called out," Robin snapped.

"No, no. Somebody told me I assumed too much," he remarked.

Her lips tightened and she dropped to her knees beside him, round face holding a half pout. "I changed my mind," she muttered. He rose up on one elbow, let his powerful thighs fall open. Robin swallowed, took the nightdress and flung it off over her head, all but leaped onto him. "Damn, Fargo, it's all I've thought about all day," she breathed, her mouth pressing onto his, her hands pushing at his shorts, pushing them down.

He turned, brought her onto her back, and caressed the two very round breasts with his hands. Her body began to press hard against him, began little pumping motions, messages of the flesh, entreaties of the loins. Her thighs opened, closed around his powerful leg, rubbed back and forth against it, eager wanting in every bodily message. He smiled down at her, eyes closed, as she enjoyed his mouth sucking on her breasts. Her lovemaking fitted her pert, pug-nosed little face, he decided, fiery, aggressive, filled with chunky energy. And now charged with new discovery, she cried out as much in joy as in pleasure, in eagerness as much as ecstasy as she pushed with him, welcomed his throbbing entry with squeals of excitement, small screams of passion, and the night wrapped itself around their lovemaking until finally, exhausted, she lay beside him, drawing in deep breaths, a little smile playing across her face with smug satisfaction, the aftermath of pleasure.

She finally sat up and Fargo enjoyed the loveliness of her exuberant, firm body, still filled with its own vibrations. "I'd best be getting back," she said, reaching for the nightdress. He nodded, the moon past the midnight sky, starting its downward slide across the blue-velvet heavens. She paused to glance at him, a sudden frowning on her face. "Only one thing that bothers me. You spoil a girl for anyone else, I'm thinking," she said.

He half shrugged. "You know what it ought to be like now. That's more than many women ever come to find out," he said. She nodded, blew him a kiss, and hurried down the slope; he lay back as her footsteps faded from earshot. He fell asleep quickly. Tomorrow would be a new day with a far different night, he was certain.

He woke when the sun splattered its yellowness against the trees, washed, and rode down to where Tom Craft served morning coffee. He'd just finished his cup when Eden appeared in the black shirt and skirt, the white sash holding the quirt. She led her horse, her face icy with anger, and her eyes speared him with blue-fire barbs.

"I want to talk to you," she hissed. "Alone." She swung onto the horse, wheeled the mount, rode a dozen yards, waited, and flashed fury at him. He rose, climbed onto the Ovaro, and followed her as she rode another dozen yards into the trees, spun the horse to face him as he came up.

"You got a bur up your rear?" he asked, feeling his own irritation at her attitude.

"I came to talk to you last night," she said. "I know now why you wanted that little piece of baggage along."

Fargo let his brows lift in mild surprise. "Eavesdropping one of your things, Eden?"

"I didn't need to eavesdrop. Her cries were quite unmistakable," Eden said icily.

"Thanks." Fargo let a modest smile touch his face.

"Dammit, I didn't come out here to compliment you," Eden flung back, her fury rising another notch.

"Oh?" he said innocently. "My mistake."

Her fury spiraled further. "I came to tell you to send her packing. Get rid of her, now, this instant."

"Thought we'd been through that," Fargo said calmly.

"I only suspected then. Now I know."

"You've got to get hold of that jealousy of yours, honey," Fargo said. He saw her hand come up to smash against his face, easily parried the blow, and watched her eyes blaze blue fire at him.

"Jealousy's nothing to do with it. I'm paying for all your time, mind, and energy and that's what I want. You want fun and games, you wait till the drive's done, till you've done your job," she said.

"I'll do my job. What else I do and when I do it is my business, honey," Fargo said, his voice turning hard.

"She goes," Eden screamed.

"She stays," Fargo said with unshakable calmness.

"You're fired," she flung at him. "Get out. You can spend all your time with her now."

"Whatever you say, honey," he said calmly. He turned the pinto and started up the hillside.

"Where are you going?" she called.

"Want to look around before I take Robin and Amos with me," he called back with unruffled calm. He sent the pinto into a trot, guided him up the steep slope, halted after he'd gone a few hundred yards. He waited, not more than a few minutes, when he heard the sound of the horse crashing through brush, pulling hard up the slope. He was dismounted when she came in sight and he marveled how she managed to look ice cool after riding hard.

"Thought you said all you had to say," he commented.

"Damn you, Fargo. You know better," she said.

"Do I? Tell me more."

"You know I can't throw you out, not now. I'd do it but I need you."

"More than you know," Fargo said. She paused, caught something in his words but decided to dismiss it.

"Just keep her out of my way," Eden said.

"Get hold of yourself, honey. There'll be enough trouble along the way without you making any," Fargo told her.

She met the harshness in his eyes without flinching. "I guess there's nothing more to say," she returned. "For now."

"For now," he agreed, and swung onto the Ovaro to ride back with her. The cattle were restless, pushing forward on their own as he returned to the campsite. Eden veered off to take charge.

"Let them move out," she ordered, began to help pull the herd together.

"Keep them on the track between the hills," Fargo called to her. He turned, rode to where Amos and Robin waited.

"What was that all about?" Robin questioned.

He decided there was nothing but bad feelings to be gained by the truth. "She wanted to continue last night's argument," he answered. "You and Amos stick with the herd. I'm going to be moving back and forth on my own today."

Amos questioned with a quick glance but Fargo rode away, climbed up the mountainside, leveled off halfway up to move forward. His eyes swept the low ground where the herd would be moving along, the passage still wide enough, and he rode on to see the passageway veer south. He rode on, following it with eyes straining, and the route turned east again and began to dip. He rode further, saw it dipped into a distant, tree-filled draw. He halted, let thoughts race through his mind, finally made decisions. No great ones, he admitted silently, but the only ones around, and he turned the pinto and rode back the way he'd come. It would take at least another day to reach the thickly forested draw and he grunted in satisfaction at the thought.

The sound of the herd rumbling along below rolled up the mountainside to him, the heavy tree cover hiding them from sight. He continued, west, in the opposite direction, finally paused to let his eyes sweep along the land to the rear. He watched, eyes narrowed, slowly wound his way down from the hillside, crossed the passageway to climb part way up the opposite hill, and turned a wide half circle, moved down again. He rode slowly, searched along the sides of the passage where the steers had trampled the grass and earth. He reined up, eyes glued to the ground, a thin smile touching his lips. He turned, climbed back up on the hillside before moving forward, stayed on high ground until the afternoon wore on and he finally rejoined the herd.

Eden called a halt where a small brook meandered across the path and let the steers drink, pushing the first ones on so the others could get to the water. She was at the head of the herd, Rob Boyson and Howie near when he reached her, his eyes moving past her to focus on a not-too-distant low ridge. She turned, followed his eyes, as did the two men, and he heard the sharp intake of her breath.

"Shit," Rob Boyson gasped out.

The row of bronzed, near-naked horsemen lined

the nearby ridge, some with lances, most with bows, their eyes focused on the herd. Fargo counted twenty as Amos came up to him.

"Are they going to attack?" Eden asked, her voice touched with fear.

"No," Fargo said. "They're giving us a warning, telling us they are there."

"Why?"

He shrugged. "Can't say. Maybe to tell us to stay away from the river." His eyes traveled slowly across the line of Indians. "Blackfoot, all of them."

"You satisfied now those Cree you saw were just a raiding party?" she asked.

"Nope," he grunted. "I saw them patrolling the river."

"There are none up there, you just said so yourself," she returned.

"On purpose," Fargo said, his eyes still on the line of red warriors. "The Cree are staying low."

"You're letting your imagination run off with you." Eden sniffed. Fargo saw the line of bronzed horsemen turn slowly as one to vanish down the far side of the ridge, as silently as they had appeared. "I was going to make camp here," Eden said, glancing at the gathering dusk.

"Go ahead. They're not going to bother us. They did what they came to do, let us see them."

She signaled for the men and began the task of getting the herd together for the night. Fargo felt the puff of hot wind, then another. It blew again, in gusts—disturbing, annoying bursts. The cattle picked up on it at once and he saw them move restlessly, the task of rounding them into a single mass for the night instantly more difficult. But it was done and the night dropped over the mountains and the meal was taken quickly, the men in small groups. He saw them take their bedrolls, prepare to sleep at once, bodies weary from the day's herding. His eyes lingered on Eden as she took her things and went to the far side of the area, an isolated, lone spot.

The dark deepened as the small cooking fire was doused and he glimpsed Eden go behind a thick bottlebrush buckeye to change, step from behind the bush a few minutes later. She seemed to be wearing a pajama outfit as she folded herself into her bedroll. Fargo got to his feet as Robin appeared. "Not tonight, honey," he said, not ungently. "Got work to do."

Her frown was instant. "You expecting trouble?" she asked.

He smiled. "Expecting anything . . . except you," he said, patted her firm little rear, and sent her off, the frown of disappointment clinging to her. He moved on foot up the slope, made his way across the slanted ground to where he could see Eden's bedroll. He moved down, on a level with her, but pushed back in the brush. The gusty puffs of hot wind continued to blow and he heard the restlessness of the herd. The night riders would have their work cut out for them this night, he pondered. He stretched out on his stomach, let his head rest on his forearm, and closed his eyes, let the world become a thing made only of sounds. It never ceased to amaze him how everything became suddenly magnified, one sensory function taking over for another. The hum of cicadas was suddenly loud; the crickets almost seemed to screech, and he caught the swishing sound of a bat as it swooped through the night. A sharp sound marked a possum moving nearby and he smelled the musky odor of a badger. A little over two hours passed by, the camp hard asleep, when he caught the sound, underbrush being pressed down, a stealthy sound, carefully spaced. It meant only one thing to the Trailsman—human footsteps—and his head lifted slowly, his gaze focusing on the sleeping figure under the blanket. He saw the brush move just beyond her head, watched, and rose to one knee. His eyes were fixed on the brush as the figure came into sight, pushing from the foliage.

The man moved silently once he was out of the brush and Fargo grunted silently. He'd made no mistake, figured the man's moves almost perfectly. Allgood, in a crouch, moved toward the figure, and Fargo rose to his feet when he saw the dull glint of the knife in the man's hand. He cursed silently as Allgood reached Eden's figure and dropped down. Fargo saw him press the knife to her throat as he clamped a hand over her mouth. The blanket jumped as Eden snapped awake, quieted at once as Allgood held the edge of the knife at her throat. Fargo saw him take his other hand from her mouth, yank her to her feet, and swing behind her in one quick motion, never taking the knife from against her throat. Holding the blade to her from behind, Allgood pushed her into the bushes, moved on, and Fargo, the Colt in his hand, moved on swift silent steps through the brush, fell in behind them. He heard Allgood pushing Eden before him, far enough from the camp now to use his voice. "Scream and it'll be your last one, bitch," he heard the man rasp.

Fargo stayed crouched, following the sound, and heard Allgood halt. "This'll do just fine," the man growled, and Fargo heard Eden's body hit the ground, heard her small gasp of pain. He increased speed, came in sight of the small circle in the forest where moonlight drifted down onto the cleared spot. Eden, in pink pajamas, bottoms that ballooned, and a loose top, lay on the ground on her elbows, facing Allgood. Her eyes held fear but fury, also. "You're gonna learn a lesson, girlie," Allgood growled.

"You're a bigger fool than I thought, coming back here," Eden snapped. "You're not scaring me into anything."

Fargo grunted in reluctant admiration. No false bravado for her; she refused to panic. "Nobody does what you did to me, bitch," Allgood snarled.

"Scum." Eden tried to turn and push herself to her feet. Allgood's hand shot out, grasped one ankle, and yanked. She came toward him along the ground, the pajama top pushing upward to reveal a glimpse of full, large breasts before she pulled it down. She tried to kick but he twisted her ankle and she gasped in pain.

Fargo had expected Allgood to try to terrify her into giving him full pay for the trip. He'd been willing to let the man scare her enough to have it stay with her and make her think twice next time before moving in. But suddenly Allgood tore his trousers open. Fargo had misjudged the man. Pussy, not pay, was on his mind.

"I'm gonna screw you into the ground, baby. I'm gonna shove it right through that high-toned ass of yours," Allgood snarled.

Fargo drew the Colt .45 and pushed from the brush. "That's all, mister," he said. Allgood froze, held the moment, then dived onto Eden, and Fargo saw the knife pressing into her throat. Allgood, spread-eagled atop her, turned his head to rasp back at Fargo.

"I'll cut her damn head off. Back off, put the gun away."

Fargo saw the line deepening into Eden's long, lovely throat and her eyes round with terror, then took a step backward and dropped the Colt into its holster. Allgood fell to one side, pulled Eden with him, came up behind her again, the knife this time pointed into her abdomen. "One wrong move and I'll stick it right through her," he warned. "Drop the gunbelt."

Fargo pulled the buckle open, let the belt slide to the ground. He hadn't wanted to fire, anyway, afraid the single shot, a sudden explosion of sound in the night, would trigger the already restless herd into a bellowing stampede.

"Kick it over here," Allgood said.

Fargo kicked the gunbelt, sideways, into the brush.

"Sonofabitch," Allgood swore.

"Never had a good sense of direction," Fargo said. He took a step forward. "Let her go and you can ride out of here," he said.

"You givin' me orders, Fargo?" Allgood frowned. "I'll cut your damn guts out, too."

"Come on, try it," Fargo said.

Allgood's sour mouth twitched, quivered. He wanted to answer the challenge but his instincts told him to take care, this was no ordinary challenger. He moved back, kept the point of the knife on Eden's abdomen. "I'll stick her, Fargo," he warned. "Another step and she gets it."

Fargo paused, thoughts racing, decided to goad the man again. He slid another step forward. "Come on, take me. You've got the knife, all the odds on your side, come on." He slid another step. "You're a stinking coward, Allgood," he sneered.

The man's mouth twitched again, harder, a little trickle of spittle coming from one corner, but he kept the knife on Eden's abdomen. It hadn't worked. It had backfired, Fargo cursed silently. Allgood was a coward, no question of that, but with a coward's sense of self-preservation. The knife was not enough of an advantage, not with someone who could challenge it as if with impunity. "Back off," he heard Allgood snarl. "Lay down, on your belly." Fargo didn't move. "On your belly or I'll ram it through her," the man shouted. He pushed the knife tip for emphasis and Fargo heard Eden's sharp cry of pain, saw a tiny spot of red appear on the pajama where the knife tip rested against her.

Fargo stepped back, turned, lowered himself to the ground, stretched out on his stomach. "Hands over your head," Allgood ordered. Fargo obeyed as his thoughts whirled. He knew exactly what the man planned. Allgood was taking no chances, giving himself that final advantage. He'd come with Eden still at knifepoint, holding the blade on her till he was standing over the prone figure. The man would pause and gather himself, Fargo thought, then fling Eden aside and plunge the knife into his back, all in one, swift motion.

But there would be one instant, one split second between the time he had to fling Eden aside and plunge the knife downward into the prone figure at his feet. It would be no more than that, an instant. But it would have to do. He had to be ready. He tightened his every muscle, drew powerful thighs into cords of muscle. He lay still, closed his eyes to shut out all sight, all movement, all distraction. He had to make everything into the world of sound again.

He waited and the few moments seemed ages.

Then he heard Allgood move toward him, Eden's steps pushed along the ground. He lay motionless, eyes shut, listening, traced the man's progress and heard him halt, knew he was standing beside him, the knife still on Eden. He heard her breath—quick, tiny gasps—and then the moment exploded with the suddenness he expected. He heard Eden flung aside, a sudden rustle of her pajamas, and a quick, sharp gasp. Fargo threw himself sideways, every corded muscle uncoiling. He felt the knife scrape his side as the blade plunged downward.

He rolled once more, heard Allgood's curse as the blade dug into only grass and soil. He leaped to his feet and kicked out in one motion as Allgood pulled the knife from the ground. But the man reacted in time to get one shoulder up. He took the kick and went sprawling. Fargo came after him at once, started to dive at him, but Allgood sliced with the knife in a sidearm arc. Fargo pulled back as the blade just missed his stomach. The man regained his feet, came in swinging the knife, slashing the air with short, vicious motions.

Fargo backed away, caught a glimpse of the small eyes. More than rage in them, he saw—fear, too, the kind of fear that would push him into mistakes. He kept moving backward and Allgood increased his pace, darted closer, grew bolder, using the knife in longer, wider slashes. Fargo turned, tried to dart under a slash, but the man was quick and he had to twist away as the knife whistled past his ear. "You're dead, Fargo," Allgood snarled. "You and her both." He lunged; Fargo ducked the blow and the man's lips drew back in a vicious grin. He tasted victory, suddenly overwhelmed with new confidence. The big man wasn't a challenge after all.

It was the moment Fargo had waited for. He stepped backward again, seemed to stumble and fall, twisted sideways. Allgood leaped in, a short, triumphant snarl falling from his lips, the knife raised to plunge it into his victim. But instead of a man off balance, helpless, he met Fargo's arm uncoiling with the power and speed of a piledriver. The blow, backhanded, caught him alongside the jaw and the power of it sent him crashing sideways to the ground. He kept hold of the knife, started to turn, bring the blade up. But Fargo came around, followed through with a leaping twist of his body. His fist came down on the back of Allgood's neck like a sledgehammer. The man pitched forward to the ground and Fargo heard the guttural cry of pain as Allgood slowly rolled onto his back, his hand still closed around the hilt of the knife that had plunged into his belly.

Fargo watched the man's lips come open as he tried to utter sounds but only a line of red trickled from between them. Allgood made a last effort to pull the blade free but it was in too deeply and his remaining strength too little. He shuddered away the last of his life and lay still. Fargo turned to see Eden pushing herself to her feet, her eyes wide, round, almost colorless. He walked over to her, saw her bring her eyes to him, blink, let a quick shudder of breath escape her.

"It's over," he said, and she nodded, straightened, and he watched how quickly she composed herself.

"How did you manage to be here?" she asked.

"I was waiting for him to show," he said. Her brows lifted. "He's been tailing us all day."

"You expected that, didn't you?"

He nodded. "You should have. You set it up to happen. His kind would hit back."

The pale blue eyes stayed on his own. "I'm grateful to you, I really am," she said, choosing her words with care. "You're obviously used to women showing their gratefulness to you in a certain way. I won't be doing that, of course."

"And what way is that?" he asked blandly.

"You know exactly what I mean, falling into bed with you. I won't be showing my gratefulness that way."

"They don't fall into bed with me because they're grateful," Fargo said and her fine eyebrows arched in question. "They're grateful afterward," he said, and saw her eyes narrow.

"What happened won't stop me from speaking my mind, either," she said.

"Me neither." He halted at her bedroll. His hand reached out, curled around the back of her long neck, the alabaster skin very smooth to his touch. "Don't think about being grateful," he said. "Just think about wanting." He stepped back, tossed her a quick grin, and walked into the darkness, felt her eyes following him.

He took his bedroll, found a spot on the slope over the herd, and was asleep in minutes. When morning came he rose rested, washed, and joined the others in time for coffee. He'd just finished when Eden appeared. She'd chosen the black shirt, black skirt, and the white sash again, the quirt tucked into the sash. His eyes danced as she came up to him, nodded pleasantly.

"Nice outfit that, but it makes you look severe," he said. "You saying something?" He laughed.

He saw a rare moment of frustration catch at her. "No, no, of course not," she answered. His smile stayed. "You don't believe me."

He shrugged. "Question is, who are you saying it

to? Me or yourself?" He left her staring after him. He was tightening the cinch on the pinto when Robin came up, Amos sauntering after her.

"What happened last night?" she asked.

"Allgood came back for a surprise visit," Fargo said. "But he's gone now, permanently."

"He came after Eden Patterson, didn't he?" Robin said. "You expected it." Fargo nodded. "She manage to say thank you?" Robin sniffed.

"Just about." He laughed, swung onto the pinto, and rode away, stayed at a fast canter as he put distance between himself and the herd. He had scouted the passage yesterday, absorbed the turns and hard spots and the direction of it. He didn't need to do that again. This time his eyes searched for other signs and he found them soon enough, first the trail of hoof prints that crossed the way, then the little movements in the trees ahead. He halted, let the others come up to him, and motioned to Eden. She detached herself from the front of the herd and rode to where he waited.

"Ride some with me," he said. She fell alongside him as he hurried the pinto forward.

"What is it?" she asked.

"Saw the signs. I think McMurtree's ready to make his move. I want him to come talk, first. I'm thinking that when he sees you he'll come talk. He'd be expecting your pa."

"Yes, he would," Eden agreed. "But he holds no brief for me. Why do you want to talk to him?"

"I want to buy some time."

"For what?"

"For getting to a place where we can make a stand and win." He saw her eyes move back and forth, suddenly apprehensive. "Just ride nice and easy," he said. The herd was back, but close enough to be smelled and heard, which was what he wanted. He rode in silence beside Eden, almost a half hour passing before he caught the movement at the trees on the left, some fifty yards ahead. His hand rested casually on the butt of the big Colt in its holster as he rode, and suddenly the line of horsemen moved into sight, down from the left side of the high land. He watched four riders come out first, turn to face them, another group follow, swing in behind the first four. "Fourteen," he murmured to Eden.

A broad-faced man on a gray gelding pushed forward a few paces, a heavy jaw and bloodshot blue eyes, a face that was familiar with a whiskey bottle. The man waited till Fargo and Eden halted only a few feet from him. His eyes fastened on Eden. "Where's Roy? Back with the herd?"

"He's at the ranch. Broke his hip. I'm taking the herd through," Eden answered.

McMurtree's brows lifted. "The world's full of surprises," he said slowly. His smile held a nasty note in it. "This'll make for easier pickings," he said, turned to one of the men beside him, a long, narrow-bodied man with a dour face. Fargo watched McMurtree's eyes swing to him, take in his muscled body, the steel in his eyes. "Who're you?"

"Fargo, Skye Fargo," the Trailsman said. "Riding trail for Miss Eden."

"The trail's at an end, Fargo," McMurtree barked, chuckled. His eyes returned to Eden. "I'm surprised Roy sent you. Word was out that I'd be waiting. He must've heard it. Not much stays secret."

"He knew," Eden said. "He figured you weren't much."

McMurtree's bloodshot eyes hardened, turned to

Fargo. "You can pull out with your skin now, Fargo. I'm taking that herd, payment for what's owed me."

"Nothing's owed you, McMurtree," Eden cut in. "Nobody cheated you out of anything. You just made up a good excuse for cattle rustling."

The man's eyes stayed on him, Fargo noticed. "Your chance, big man," he said. "Cut out now or catch a bullet," he said.

"Nobody's afraid of you, McMurtree. You've always been a blowhard," Eden spit out at the man. McMurtree turned to her, his face darkening, and Fargo cut in, his eyes on Eden.

"Go on back with the others, Miss Eden," he said.

"What?" Eden frowned at him.

"Go back with the others. I want to talk with Mr. McMurtree alone," he said.

He saw Eden's surprise, uneasiness, uncertainty about what he was doing. He wanted that. It made her reactions honest. "You've nothing to say about what happens, Fargo," she said.

"We'll talk about that later," he said. "Just go back with the others, Eden. For me. Just do it."

Eden frowned at him, tried to read his eyes and failed. Her lips bit down onto each other and her lovely face flushed, but she whirled the horse and galloped away.

"Always a tough gal," McMurtree said. Fargo saw the hardness in the man's eyes. "No deals, Fargo. I'm taking the herd, all of it. I could take it right now."

"You'd lose a lot of men that way. It'd be a free-for-all," Fargo said. "My way's better."

"What's your way?" the man asked.

"I want time, twenty-four hours, to convince Eden not to go down fighting," Fargo said.

"Convince her? Not that one," McMurtree said.

"Give me the night with her," Fargo said, leaving the rest hanging. McMurtree picked up on it at once.

"So that's the way it is," he said, his brows lifting. "I knew somebody would get her sometime."

"Back off. Don't let her think you're waiting to rush us. Let me have the night, my way," Fargo said. "You can always come in shooting if I don't get anywhere."

The man's lips pursed. "That's true enough," he said. "I like the easy way if it's possible. Twenty-four hours won't make a difference. You've got the night to save her ass, Fargo. You can kiss it and save it all at once," he roared, exploded in coarse laughter as he wheeled his horse in a circle. Fargo watched him lead his men into the trees, traced his path up by the movement of the branches. McMurtree moved on, headed for the high ground, and Fargo turned the pinto back to meet the herd.

Eden waited with eyes as cold as a mountain spring as he rode up. "I hope you've an explanation," she snapped.

"The best kind. It worked. I bought us twenty-four hours."

"How?" she demanded.

"I let him think I could convince you to back down," Fargo told her. "I let on I had a special way with you."

"What do you really figure to do?" she questioned icily.

"We go on till night, camp as usual. I'll give you the rest when the time comes." His eyes swept the men who had gathered to listen.

"I told them," Eden said, anticipating his question.

"You think we've a chance, Fargo?" Tom Craft

100

asked, and Fargo saw Eden catch the meaning behind the question. They were looking to him for answers, angered because she hadn't come clean with them till now.

"We'll have a chance. We'll set them up and bushwhack them," Fargo said.

"We're one gun short," Howie said with a quick, resentful glance at Eden. Her face remained like ice.

"We'll make do," Fargo said. "Start moving the herd, the faster the better. Take them along this passage as far as you can get before night."

The men turned to their tasks at once and he saw Eden join with them. He swung the pinto and rode point. Eden drove herself as hard as any of the men and he didn't call a rest break, kept the herd driving on. He estimated they were only a few miles from where he wanted to be when night slid over the mountains and he was satisfied. The herd milled restlessly but under control along the passageway as Tom Craft broke out enough for a quick meal.

"You've four hours to sleep," Fargo said. "Until midnight. Make the most of it."

The others found spots to lay down, weariness doing the rest at once, and he saw Amos and Robin against a far tree. He stretched out as Eden came to him.

"Why till midnight, Fargo? I want some answers," she said.

"We move again at midnight," he said. "There's a draw only a mile or two further on."

"A draw? We'll be trapped there," she said.

"It's very thick with trees," he said.

"Worse," she snapped.

"No, better. We don't want the herd stampeded.

101

That won't happen there. Too thick with trees. All they'll be able to do is mill around and run into each other. There'll be no room for them to get themselves into a stampede charge."

"McMurtree will pick up the trail come morning."

"He can't miss it. He'll figure I sold him a bill of goods and come charging after us. He'll think we went and trapped ourselves when he sees the draw and come charging in," Fargo said.

"We'll be waiting," she finished.

"And ready. We take him and the herd can't stampede."

She gave him a long, appraising glance. "Sounds as though it might just work," she said. "By God, it really does, the way you lay it out."

"If your crew can shoot straight. Every damn shot has to count."

"Don't say it again. We're one gun short." She frowned. "Or two guns up," she added, and he waited. "The old man and the girl," she said.

"That little piece of baggage?" Fargo frowned. "And that old man who's only good for polishing boots?"

He watched her lips tighten, the pale blue eyes fasten on him. "They'll fight if you ask them," she said.

"You want their help? You ask them," he tossed back.

"You push hard, don't you?"

"You deserve it. It's time you had to eat some of your damn bitchy words."

She lapsed into silence and pushed herself to her feet, walked to where Robin and Amos were on their blankets. Fargo turned on his side, and with hearing that could match a cougar's, picked up her voice as she halted, met Robin's hostile stare, Amos's quiet waiting.

"Fargo says it's all or nothing," Eden began. "We'll need every gun we can get, you included." Fargo heard her pause, draw in a deep breath. "I don't expect you to do it for me. I haven't made you feel exactly welcome," she continued, and he heard Robin's snort of derisive agreement. "Do it for yourselves, for Fargo, or maybe because it's the right thing to do. McMurtree is a lizard, nothing more. He'll slaughter us all if he has to."

"What if we say no thank you?" Robin asked.

"Ride out now, tonight. You'll be far enough away by morning. I won't blame you."

Fargo listened to the long moment of silence, heard Amos's voice answering for Robin and himself. "We'll do our part," Amos said. "No great choice but I'd rather be shot than scalped."

"Thank you," Eden said, her voice low, quiet, and Fargo watched her return, back straight, her face tight but without the usual ice in it when she reached him, a tiredness in the pale blue eyes.

"I heard," Fargo said.

"No comments?" she asked with an edge.

"Not the best apology I ever heard but all right for a first time."

"I don't expect to have to perfect the technique," she said frostily, strode away, and ignored his grin. He lay back and closed his eyes. Midnight would come too quickly.

5

Fargo watched the men cut out a quarter of the herd at his directions. The smaller number could be moved more quickly and more quietly. He left Eden to see over the rest of the herd, took three men, and led the first batch of steers along the passageway until, some two miles on, he reached the draw.

"Pack them in," he said, left one man to stay with them, and returned with the other two. The draw was as thickly forested as he'd thought, and he grunted in satisfaction. He had Tom Craft lead the second batch of steers, Eden the last. Amos and Robin paused alongside him as he rode tail after the last of the steers.

"You had to twist her arm, didn't you?" Robin said.

"Not much," he answered. "She's learning."

"You figure to teach her anything else?" Robin asked petulantly.

"You figure to let me?" He grinned.

"Like hell," she snapped, and rode off. Amos followed, shaking the thatch of white hair atop the parchment face. Fargo followed the herd to the draw, helped in pushing the animals as deep as possible into the area. He saw the pink line of dawn touching the mountains. Night and the need for quiet had taken time but the herd all but filled the heavily wooded draw now, jammed in among white pine, balsam, cedar, and hackaberry, pressed against the trees, standing restlessly in all directions. If they panicked, they'd only run into each other and jam up against the trunks.

The men gathered, Robin and Amos to one side. "Pick a spot, both sides of the draw. Three of you go up into the woods," Fargo said. "I'll fire the first shot and then you pour it into them. Pick your targets, no wasted shooting." His eyes traveled across the men, lingered on Robin. "Anybody gets squeamish about mowing them down, just remember they came to do the same to you. McMurtree won't leave anyone behind. A cattle rustler can't afford to do that."

The men nodded, began to fan out. He saw Rob Boyson, Howie, and Tom Craft take to the trees, disappear high up in the thick foliage of red cedars. Robin and Amos settled down out of sight behind a thick stand of butterfly bushes.

Only Eden remained and he saw her eyes on him. "Where are you going?" she asked.

"Right here, behind these hackaberries. That way we'll pour it into them from three sides," he said. She nodded and moved behind the tree next to him. He slid down behind his own tree, settled himself with the big Sharps cradled in one arm. The wait was shorter than he'd expected, the sound of hoofbeats at a full gallop echoing along the passage. He shifted position, rose on one knee, the rifle raised, and he saw Eden bring up her gun.

The horses came into view, going full out, McMurtree in the lead, the narrow, long-figured man to his left. "There they are, the sonofabitches," he heard McMurtree shout as the man caught sight of the draw and the steers filling almost every inch of it. "The stupid bastards got themselves trapped. Wipe 'em out," McMurtree shouted in glee.

Fargo's smile was a thing of grim satisfaction. He'd read McMurtree perfectly; the man was a bullheaded fool, too caught up in his own rage to even consider caution. Fargo raised the big Sharps to his shoulder, aimed at McMurtree as the man led the charge into the draw. He fired just as McMurtree ducked his head to pass under a low branch. Fargo saw the shot blow the man's hat off, McMurtree's bloodshot eyes growing wide as he pulled back on his horse. The volley of shots exploded, echoing in the draw to sound as though a small army were hidden there. Fargo saw four of McMurtree's men topple from their horses almost as one and the others rein up, wheel, surprise and fear flooding over them. Three more riders fell, shots blasting one out of his saddle as though he'd been yanked off by invisible strings.

McMurtree, head low, started to race for the side of the draw and Fargo swung the Sharps, fired. The shot struck the man in the shoulder and Fargo saw him rise, clutch at his arm as he fell out of the saddle. The rest of his men had started to fire back but they were shooting aimlessly into trees and brush, and he saw one start to race away and manage no more than a dozen feet before two shots tore his chest apart.

McMurtree, on the ground, his face a mask of fear, tried to run a zigzag course, one hand clutching his shoulder. Fargo heard the steers crashing into each other, bellowing, moving against the trees, and two of McMurtree's men managed to reach the entrance to the draw and flee up the passageway. McMurtree had disappeared into the brush, and the sound of gunfire abruptly ended. There were no targets left, Fargo saw as he rose, and Tom Craft and Howie dropped out of the trees, Rob Boyson following.

"McMurtree, come out," Fargo shouted. "It's over." He waited, saw the others begin to emerge from their hiding places. His eyes swept the bushes. "Don't be stupid, McMurtree. Come out," he called again. "It's over. You can go in one piece."

He heard the sudden sharp cry, Robin's voice. "It's not over, you lying bastard," he heard McMurtree shout. "My gun's in this little lady's back right now." Fargo swore silently. The man had circled, found himself behind Robin and Amos, and seized his chance. "Everybody lines up and throws their guns down or I'll blow her apart," McMurtree shouted from behind the brush.

Fargo glanced at the others, saw their eyes on him. "Do as he says," Fargo told them, and moved out to line up in front of the others. Eden came alongside him, let her rifle fall to the ground. Slowly, Robin came through the brush, McMurtree close behind her, the gun in the small of her back.

"An exchange, Fargo, you lyin' sonofabitch. I want Eden Patterson," McMurtree said. "I want her or this one is a dead filly." Fargo saw Eden's eyes go to him, the round orbs even paler with fear.

"Why?" Fargo asked.

"Roy Patterson can ransom his bitch daughter back. I figure she'll be worth more than the herd," the man said. "You just bring her over here. No tricks. I got a very itchy trigger finger and my shoulder hurts bad where you winded me."

Fargo looked at Eden, saw the tightness in her face, her eyes a turmoil of emotions. His gaze flicked to Robin, saw the terror and pleading in the brown eyes.

"Make up your damn mind. You got thirty seconds more," the man shouted.

Fargo opened his lips to answer when Eden's voice cut in. "Let her go," Eden said as she started toward where the man held Robin. She cast a quick glance back at Fargo, a wry smile touching her lips, something close to forgiveness in her eyes, and then she looked away, walked on, her back very straight, her long, supple figure beautifully composed. McMurtree waited till she'd reached him. He flung Robin to the ground and pressed the gun into Eden's neck with one quick motion.

"Anybody follows me, I kill her. You can count on it," the man said as he backed into the brush. Fargo listened to him making a wide circle, stayed motionless, his eyes sweeping the others.

"He means it," Fargo warned. "Everybody stay where you are. Give him time to put distance between himself and us. He'll find some of the horses that ran out of here and be on his way."

Robin pushed to her feet and rushed over to him, her face still ashen. "Goddamn," he heard Tom Craft say. "Doesn't seem right, just letting him go off with Eden."

"You heard him. You go flying after him and she's dead," Fargo answered.

"Still doesn't seem right, us doing nothing," the man said.

"Get the herd out of here. We'll have to back the way we came. Getting to this draw took us out of our way." Fargo said.

Tom Craft stared at him. "You going to take the herd through as if nothing happened?"

"He's going after her," Fargo heard Robin blurt out, casting an impatient glance at Tom Craft. "His way, his time, because he's the only one with any chance of saving her neck. Right, Fargo?"

Fargo smiled slowly. "How'd you get so smart?" he asked Robin.

"It's not being smart. It's being a woman."

He laughed, turned to the others. "Start getting that herd out." He saw the men jump to work with eagerness. He pitched in, helped in the long, slow task of cutting the steers out of the trees, untangling knots of frightened, stubborn animals, finally heading them back along the passageway between the mountains. It took most of the day. As he watched dusk settling in, he turned to Tom Craft. "Make camp anywhere that seems a good spot." He turned the pinto and hurried away with a wave to Robin. She watched with her round face unsmiling. He moved into the tree cover, certain that McMurtree hadn't risked riding out into the relative clear of the passageway. It took him too long but he finally picked up the trail, two horses, moving slowly. They'd halted by a small brook and he saw red-stained pieces of shirt. McMurtree had cleaned his wound, put on fresh bandages. He saw a torn piece of black cloth hanging from a branch and knew what McMurtree had used as bandages.

He followed, the trail easy enough to pick up again. McMurtree was moving slowly and Fargo saw he was close as the night closed in, the hoof prints fresh and soft. He continued on in the darkness, pausing often to feel the ground with his fingers, lift his nose, draw deeply of the night air. A wind had come up, cooling, and suddenly his nostrils twitched as he caught the scent of horses to his left, a few hundred yards on, he guessed. He dismounted and moved forward on foot as the moon came up enough to cast a pale light. The scent grew stronger and he caught sound of a horse blowing air.

He changed directions as the horse blew air again, ten degrees to his right, and crept forward as the dim moon filtered through enough to outline the figures in front of him. He saw Eden first, tied to a tree with a rope around her neck that gave her no place to move. She'd taken what was left of the black blouse and fashioned a kind of halter that covered her breasts with more effort than success. McMurtree sat against a nearby tree, head down, asleep, the black blouse bandage on his shoulder. Fargo frowned. The man had taken his boots off and propped a rifle up at his feet, the muzzle pointed directly at Eden. All he had to do was pull the trigger and the rifle would blast her.

But the man was still a fool. Fargo frowned. All the man had to do was pull the trigger, and he seemed to think he'd have the chance. Fargo drew the big Sharps forward, raised it to his shoulder, peered along the barrel, and brought McMurtree's head into his sight, wondering whatever made the man think anyone would do otherwise. Yet he'd positioned the rifle at his feet, aimed at his captive target as if he never considered he could be blasted away before getting a chance to pull the trigger.

Fargo frowned again as he sighted along the Sharps. It didn't make sense. The man couldn't be that stupid. Something was wrong, his intuition warned him, and his finger stayed poised on the trigger. He lowered the rifle, let his eyes move over McMurtree's figure again, and suddenly heard his own silent oath.

McMurtree wasn't that complete a fool, all right. Fargo's eyes stayed riveted to the man's foot. A thin piece of string was tied around his big toe. It ran, with only the faintest bit of slack in it, to the trigger of the rifle. Fargo swore again. McMurtree had rigged up a vicious little bit of business that would make his promise come true, to kill Eden if anyone came after him. Any shot that blasted him would send his body falling or stiffening in a final spasm. The string would pull tight, the rifle fire its bullet into its helpless target. Dead or alive, McMurtree would have his promise fulfilled. Fargo cursed the man's cleverness again. An inadvertent move in his sleep wouldn't fire the gun; the trigger needed more pull than that. But a bullet slamming into his figure would be more than enough.

He shifted the big Sharps, his lips drawn back in a grimace. He'd have but one chance; Eden's life swung in the balance. His eyes sighted along the rifle barrel, focused on the spot in the string where it was knotted around McMurtree's toe. Slowly, very slowly, his finger tightened on the trigger. The shot exploded in the silence and Fargo saw the knot vanish, part of McMurtree's toe with it. He swung the rifle instantly as McMurtree leaped awake, started to bring his six-gun up to level it at Eden. The big Sharps fired again and, at that range, seemed to blow McMurtree's head from his shoulders. The man's body arched backward, as if in pursuit of its head, crashed with a thud, and lay still, half hidden by the curve of the tree trunk.

Fargo stepped from the trees, Eden's round, pale eyes upon him. He knelt beside her, used his Arkansas throwing knife to cut the rope from around her

111

neck, and she fell against him. He felt the trembling in her body. He held her, the soft tips of her breasts pressed into him. She stopped the trembling by sheer willpower, he knew, and pulled back.

"Sorry about that," she said, bringing control into her voice.

"I'm not." He smiled.

She took a few minutes more to gather herself, drew in deep breaths which made the alabaster mounds all but swell from the contrived halter. He leaned back against the tree.

"Why'd you do it?" he asked.

"Stop you from making the choice?" she returned, and he nodded, waited. "Decided to take you off the hook. You were going to make the same choice anyway, me for her, right?" He didn't answer. "No matter," she said.

"No, it does matter," he disagreed. "Go on."

She studied him for a long moment. "Not because you're mad for her," she said. "But it was my fight, my doing. She was an innocent. She oughtn't to have had to pay for it. That was for me to do."

"You're half right," he said. "But those weren't my reasons." Her brows arched in question. "They were simpler. He would've killed her right on the spot. He wanted you for ransom. You had time left, enough for me to come after you. All the rest is window dressing."

The pale blue orbs held on him and she came forward, opened her lips, pressed them on his mouth, no passion but a surprising softness. "Thank you," she said. "I thought it was over for me."

"It's only begun for you." He grinned.

Her face grew set at once. "I haven't changed my thoughts about that," she said.

He rose, pulled her to her feet. "I've faith in you," he said. "Now let's get back to the others."

"Yes, I've a herd to get through," she said, and he was reluctantly admiring of how quickly she could return to her usual self. He led the way back, reached the others as dawn broke. Eden accepted their excitement at arm's length and was totally in command in but a few minutes. Fargo had coffee, saw Robin watching Eden direct the men as they started the herd moving, disapproval in her eyes. He strolled over to Robin and her eyes flicked a quick glance at him, then returned to Eden.

"She'll never change. Nothing gets to her," Robin muttered.

"Don't buy that," Fargo said.

Robin leveled her frown at him. "You saved her neck, twice now. You think she's going to listen to you any more than she ever did? You think she's going to give in on anything?"

"That's not her way. Don't expect that," he said. "Besides, inside changing comes first. It takes longer to become different outside." He speared Robin with a narrowed glance. "She changed places with you. She could've said no. You seem to be forgetting that."

Robin's face didn't yield any. "You wouldn't have let her do anything else. She knew that," Robin snapped back, and spun away. He mounted the pinto as he marveled at the workings of the female mind and wondered if she were right.

Amos rode beside him as the herd moved back toward where they could turn east again. "You pulled this one out of the fire," Amos said. "You going to try to cross the Milk now?"

He answered, aware that Eden was more than

113

close enough to hear. "Not without checking on the Cree again."

Eden swerved her horse, was beside him at once. "You still bothered about those few Cree you saw?"

"That's right," he said.

"You still think that row of Blackfoot we saw were there to hide something?" she pressed. "You still think the Cree are lying in wait?"

"Something like that."

"You're a stubborn man."

He nodded agreement. "And usually right."

"What if you're wrong this time?"

"What if I'm not?"

Her lips pressed down onto one another as she wheeled the horse and rode away crossly.

"How do you expect to get answers and keep your scalp?" Amos asked.

"I've till morning to figure that one out." Fargo grinned as Eden called a halt near a stream. Night came quickly. He pulled his bedroll from the campsite to head up onto high ground. Eden paused as she came past, hairbrush in one hand.

"Expecting night visitors again?" she remarked, and he heard her try to hold back the acid in her voice. She was only partly successful.

"Should I be?"

The hesitation was brief, but he caught it, smiled inwardly. "No," she said. "Good night, Fargo."

He nodded, continued on, and found himself a place on a flat ledge of soft grass under a balsam. He laid out his bedroll and his body reminded him that it had been forty-eight hours of tension-packed moments since he'd slept. He lay back, was asleep at once. The moon had moved past the midnight mark when his cat's sleep ended. The footsteps were quick, hurried little movements, and he waited as Robin appeared in a long shirt and nothing else. She dropped down beside him, curled herself under the blanket with him.

"I'm still pretty damn tired," he murmured to her.

"I know that. I don't want to do anything but be beside you," she said.

"For real?" he said sleepily.

"Promise." She settled down tight against him, little-girl-like. She was asleep in moments and his exhaustion let him join her at once.

Her promise held till just before daybreak and, he realized, the breaking of it was unplanned, perhaps as much his own doing as hers. He had turned and his hand came to rest against her warm, round little rear. She sighed, moved, came onto her back. His hand slipped around to rest on the wiry triangle and seemed to slide downward with a will of its own. Robin whispered, moaned. "Aaaaah ... ooooooh ..." The sounds drifted softly to him. His fingers came to rest against the soft, damp lips and the little moan became a short gasped cry. The rest simply followed, her hips moving, positioning themselves for him, her body suddenly awake with wanting already spiraling. He answered and it seemed only right and natural, and all promises were tucked away. Her scream of ecstasy and the new sun touched the mountainside at the same time. When she finished resting against him, he sent her scurrying back down to the campsite before daylight painted the land.

He rose later, rested, unexpectedly satisfied. When he made his way down to the camp, Robin was just pulling herself from her bedroll. It was plain she'd taken another few hours of sleep and looked both rumpled and contented, her glance full of quiet smugness. He had coffee with Amos as Eden appeared, gray shirt stretched beautifully taut in front, gray riding skirt and the quirt tucked into the wide belt. She managed to seem totally cool and contained when she paused beside Fargo as he finished his coffee.

"I think you should change your mind and stop wasting time chasing down a few Crees," she said.

"I think you should go push your cows around," Fargo replied, and he saw Eden's pale blue eyes narrow.

"Damn, Fargo, we're running real late now," she flared.

"Better late than dead, I always say."

She tossed him an acid glance and strode away.

Amos's voice brought his attention back. "You figure a way last night?" he asked.

"I think so," Fargo answered. "Let's go see how good a decoy I can make." He got the pinto, saddled it, and Amos followed as he left camp in a fast trot. He headed north where the Milk River lay out of sight but shrouded by more than trees and hills. He slowed, let Amos come alongside him.

"You head up into heavy tree cover in a few minutes," he said. "Have your rifle ready to fire. I'm going to ride straight and hard right for the river."

Amos nodded. "You figure they'll come out after you."

"That's right. Soon as they come after me, you open fire and draw their attention to you. Don't bother aiming, just lay down a barrage," Fargo said. He gestured to a rock outcrop that rose in the

116

distance. "Break off firing when they start after you and head up there. We'll meet at those rocks."

"You hope," Amos said.

"I'm expecting they won't go off chasing in two directions, not knowing what they might be running up against," Fargo said.

Amos's nod carried little conviction, and with a nod of his own, Fargo sent the pinto into a gallop and drove forward. He rode hard, headed straight north toward the river, avoiding every cover that beckoned invitingly. Staying highly visible, he kept driving forward when he caught the trees shake at his left. He started to turn the pinto when the woods erupted in an explosion of lance-waving horsemen.

"Shit," he muttered as his quick glance took in at least thirty warriors, most wearing the shapeless, sleeveless shirt of the Cree, the other with Cree armbands. He spurred the pinto over the ground and uttered another oath as, almost directly in front of him, the sandbar willows disgorged another band of racing horsemen. Twenty, in the second group, he guessed.

He veered off and suddenly the rifle fire from the distant trees on the slope cut the air. He saw both bands of Cree rein in to a halt, confused for a moment. Amos did his job well, firing off volley after volley in quick succession rather than trying to aim. Fargo seized the precious seconds to increase his lead to an almost comfortable margin. He glanced back to see the second band take off in the direction of the rifle fire while the larger group started to pursue him again. But he was going full out and he heard the sound of the rifle fire abruptly cease. Amos had decided it was time to hightail it, too. He had good space between himself and the

Indians, Fargo saw. He'd have a little more as they slowed to search the trees and pick him up. He uttered a silent hope that Amos would make the most of it.

Fargo pushed the pinto hard but the horse took the climb with power and ease, leaving the shorter-legged Indian ponies further behind. He took a steep climb, bent forward in the saddle as the pinto pulled himself upward. He now headed completely away from the river, aiming straight for the high rocks. He glanced back to see the band chasing him halt, break off pursuit, and he kept on, reached the rock outcrop and reined in, the big Sharps in one hand. He waited perhaps a few minutes when he heard Amos galloping, saw the white thatch of hair appear, and his eyes peered past the onrushing horse to see the brush and the trees shaking hard. The ones after Amos hadn't pulled back; Fargo's curse was short as he wheeled the pinto, held, let Amos catch up to him.

"Bastards," he heard Amos shout as he fell in alongside the Ovaro. Fargo veered, raced through a narrow space between tall granite blocks. It would slow them a few seconds more as they'd have to pull back, follow only two at a time. The narrow passage emerged on a rock-strewn area and Fargo pulled the Ovaro to a halt, wheeled to face the end of the passageway, the big Sharps at his shoulder. He fired as the first two Cree raced out of the passage. Both Indians arched from their horses to hit the side of the granite and slide to the ground, each leaving a broad red mark along the stone. The next two tried to halt in time but Fargo's shot caught one and he bent over on his pony, hung for a moment, and then toppled to the ground. Fargo heard the shouts and the collision of horses as the others piled up in the narrow passage, the front riders unwilling to rush out and be picked off.

Fargo sent the Ovaro on across the rocky terrain, Amos at his heels, turned in behind a tall, cone-shaped boulder with a hole eroded by wind and rain at one edge that let him see down to the exit of the passageway. He aimed the rifle, saw one of the Cree try to dart out on foot. His shot caught the Indian as he was racing and the man's short scream of pain ended as he pitched head-first in a forward somersault to lay still on the hot rock flooring. Fargo waited, ears straining, and he heard the sounds of muffled commands, horses being led slowly back down the passage.

"Smart savages," Amos muttered. "They didn't pull back the way the ones chasing you did. They figured we'd be meeting someplace and they'd get us both."

"That's what they're still figuring. They'll wait down at the bottom end of the defile," Fargo said.

"They know we can't stay here long without burning up. They figure we'll have to come down and try to make a run for it," Amos said.

Fargo nodded, his brows knitting together. "They've a reason for keeping after us this way. The same reason that made them go after you and Robin's kin the way they did," he said.

"Somethin', all right, but what?" Amos said.

"We'll work on that later. First, we're getting out of here down the back side. When we reach the bottom we can circle around. It'll take us a good while but when we get back to the others we'll have our scalps on," Fargo said.

Amos moved a few paces to stare down at the steep, back side of the rocks, his eyes tracing along the narrow, almost precipitous, crag-filled passages.

Fargo watched him shake his head slowly. "Maybe you can make it," Amos said. "But my horse and me, we're too old. We don't have the strength or the footing left for that kind of going."

"I'll get you down," Fargo said. "Just wait here. I want to make sure they're settled down to wait." He took the pinto around the tall, cone-shaped boulder and back into the narrow defile, dismounted when he neared the entrance at the other end. He crept forward on foot, silent, catlike steps, crouched down to ease himself out just enough to let him scan the scene before him. The Cree, dismounted, had formed a half circle facing the entrance to the defile. They had plainly settled down to wait. His eyes moved across the line, halted at a near-naked figure in the center. The Cree wore a white-tipped golden-eagle feather in his hair, the kind the Indians called breath feathers because of their lightness. It was the mark of a leader, and this Cree was imposing-looking, with a typical broad Cree face but with a large nose that added to his eaglelike stare.

Fargo fastened the Indian's face in his mind as he backed into the defile, turned, and climbed back the way he came, leading the pinto till he was halfway up the passage. He'd seen what he came to see. The Cree had plainly settled in to wait, confident that was all they had to do. Amos rose from his seat on a rock as Fargo emerged from the defile. "We'll be long gone by the time they come aware that we're not making a break for it," Fargo said. He gestured to a small, sharp passage that ran diagonally down and across the rocks on the other side. "That's where we start," he said, taking his lariat down and tossing the one end to Amos. "Tie it around your saddle horn," he said. "Then run it from the horn to around your waist. Leave some slack in between."

Amos nodded and fastened the one end of the lariat tight around his saddle horn, mounted, and wrapped the rest around his waist. Fargo played out enough of the rope and tied the other end to his own saddle horn. "I figure the pinto and I will give your horse just enough backpull to keep his feet and his balance," he said.

" 'Less you fall," Amos grunted.

"Then we're both in trouble," Fargo agreed. "Now start down." Amos shrugged and began to guide his horse down the sharply turned path. Fargo followed, leaving some room, and Amos's horse did well until he was halfway along the path. The ground fell off further and Fargo saw the horse's hindquarters bunch up as his forefeet slipped and he tried to keep balance. Fargo felt the lariat tighten, pull on the Ovaro, and he leaned back in the saddle to add balance to the horse. The Ovaro's powerful hindquarters tightened, held, and supplied the backpull the other horse needed.

"You're all right," he called to Amos and the white thatch nodded vigorously.

The descent became sharper, the tension greater, and in mountain-climber fashion, each time Amos's horse slipped, the Ovaro provided the backpull and the balance that just kept him from falling. Fargo kept both hands on the lariat that wrapped around his saddle horn, pulled with all his strength whenever he felt it start to tighten, and leaned as far back in the saddle as he could at the same time. They weren't halfway down when he felt his back and shoulder muscles screaming in pain and he halted in gratitude at a narrow ledge of rock that suddenly appeared. There was just enough room for both horses to rest, one behind the other, and barely enough room for him to climb down from the saddle. He took a jar of wintergreen oil from his saddlebag and massaged the pinto's forelegs, then did the same with the powerful hindlegs. He felt the tension still twitching in the tensor muscle where the greatest strain occurred.

"That's some damn horse, Fargo," Amos said. "He's got himself to hold and he's holding up my mount. He must be built like a rock."

"He is, but he's feeling it. We'll take it slow, real slow," Fargo said, stopped the jar, and returned it to the saddlebag. The oil of wintergreen worked itself in fast and would continue to soothe aching muscles. Amos began the descent again. The painful progress continued, step by step, the two men resting wherever possible as the pathways grew narrower and steeper. Fargo felt the Ovaro beginning to lose his own footing, his strength ebbing. He was about to call to Amos when he saw him rein up on the narrow ledge, raise his arm.

"We've had it, Fargo," Amos called back. "No place left to go." Fargo eased the pinto forward, a few careful steps, and halted to peer past Amos. The narrow pathway had vanished. Only a steep, almost perpendicular slope remained. It fell sharply down the mountainside, heavily covered with thick scrub brush clinging onto a surface of a sandy loam. Fargo cautiously swung from the pinto, his feet resting on the very edge of the ledge. He scanned the steep slope, swore silently. There was no good way, no easy way, only the best of the bad.

"Get the rope off your saddle horn. I'll unwind mine," Fargo said as he began to undo the lariat that had almost cut into the saddle horn. When he'd finished unwinding, he pulled the rest slowly back from Amos.

"What're you figuring, big man?" Amos asked.

"We can't go back. We can't even turn. There's no way to go but down. But the horses won't make it with a rider on them and we won't make it in the saddle. They have to be free to balance themselves as best they can and that'd be impossible with a rider. They've got to be able to fall on their own if they have to. Even a saddle will upset their balance."

Amos nodded and began to unstrap his saddle, had his off as Fargo did the same. "Bridles, too, right?" he asked, and Fargo nodded as he took the bridle from the pinto and wrapped it tightly around the saddle. He looked down the precipitous slope again, met Amos's glance. The bottom seemed thick with good green brush and a long way down. He raised the saddle, checked the bridle wrapped around it, and tossed both as far as he could, watched the saddle hit the steep side, dislodge a cloud of the sandy loam, and continue tumbling downward. Amos's saddle followed, bounced along an almost parallel path. Fargo saw Amos's eyes on him and nodded back.

"Take him down," he said. "Move slow, stay as horizontal as you can. And be ready to get the hell out of the way if he starts to go."

Amos nodded understanding and Fargo hung back, watched as he moved from the end of the ledge onto the steep side of the slope. Amos kept one hand on the horse's nose, the touch aimed at calming as well as leading. He took short steps and stayed on a downward line. Fargo watched the horse dig hooves into the sandy loam, work to keep his balance, and he continued to wait and let

Amos take a good lead before he moved forward. When he did, he stepped cautiously from the last of the ledge and felt the sheer steepness of the slope at once. He kept one hand outstretched on the Ovaro's neck, urging the horse forward.

He more or less followed the path Amos had taken, felt himself lean into the slope to retain his balance. The pinto's hooves dug into the soft side of the steep drop; the horse leaned, felt the unsure footing, and grew nervous. Fargo saw it at once in the horse's eyes, felt it in the tension of the powerful neck muscles.

"Easy, boy, easy," he murmured, but he felt his own footing slide. He slipped to one knee, caught hold of a piece of brush, and pulled himself up. He halted, cast an eye forward at Amos. The man had let go of the horse, used both hands to steady himself against the slope. The horse slid, slipped, tried to dig in, and slipped again. Fargo grimaced, wanted to shout caution but there was no reason. Amos could do no more than he was doing and Fargo moved forward again, the pinto following. Once more he felt his feet go out from under him, caught himself, and saw the heavy bulk of the pinto slide, almost come down on top of him, but the horse managed to retain his footing, held steady.

Fargo frowned. The pinto should have been holding steadier than Amos's horse, yet he was having as much trouble, and Fargo peered across the steep side to where Amos continued to bring his horse along. He saw the answer as Amos's mount slid, dug in both rear hooves, and kept his balance. A small shower of the sandy loam cascaded down the steep side where both Amos and his horse dug in to keep their footing. They were loosening the already weak soil further.

Fargo moved downward to try and carve out another path along the sharply sloped soil. He'd taken but a few steps when he heard Amos's shout, alarm and fear in it. He spun to see Amos falling, the heels of his boots sending a shower of loose soil. The horse started to bolt, and Fargo saw it slide down on its side and gather speed, become a whirling, falling mass of bone and muscle. He lost sight of Amos in the cascade of loose soil that poured down the slope.

He turned back to the pinto and felt the soil under him come loose, tried to grab hold of a piece of bush, but it, too, broke away as the entire slope began to slide, a chain reaction from the soil kicked loose by Amos and his horse. Fargo had time only to see the Ovaro fall, try to maintain some balance, then go down with the loam that slid loose. His vision went skyward as he was flipped onto his back and he closed his mouth in time to avoid taking in the soil that cascaded over him. He felt himself helplessly falling, tumbling, hitting his shoulder against a piece of rock. He heard the pinto, thought he could hear Amos but wasn't sure as a world of loose soil, rock, and brush poured down over him. He grabbed some brush to slow his headlong fall, but it only came off in his hands. His legs swung sideways and he drew them up, brought his knees up high and partly formed himself into a ball. He straightened out when he saw he was gathering too much speed and cried out in sharp pain as something hard slammed against his thigh.

The soil seemed less loose now and he forced his eyes open to see the thick green bushes just below. He bounced into them, grateful for their springy softness, and felt himself tossed sideways, cushioned, falling through a space, cushioned again, and finally he lay still, swaying gently atop a thicket of heavy-leafed calico pipe.

He shook himself, tried to sit up. The bushes moved and he dropped to all fours. He pulled his way up at once, clawed through the brush to gaze up at the precipitous slope where large swaths of soil had been rolled away to give the slope dark brown stripes. He climbed further, saw movement to his right, the flash of black and white glinting through the green of the brush. He half ran, half tore his way through the brush toward the pinto, reached the horse to see him standing well on all four legs, a scraped patch of hide along his rump and a small cut on his left foreleg just above the cannon bone. He ran his hands over the horse, let him take a few steps. Other than the cuts and bruises, he seemed to have come through it all right and the big man let out a sigh of relief.

He stood, pulled his way to the top of the green brush, and scanned the bottom of the slope. What seemed a white bush moved almost at dead center of the slope and Fargo started toward it as it rose further, became Amos. The thin figure walked unsteadily and Fargo saw Amos holding his left shoulder with his right hand. Hurrying, the Ovaro following after him, he reached Amos and saw the pain in the old man's dirtied, bruised face.

"Let's have a look," Fargo said as he helped Amos down onto his knees. He moved the old man's shoulder, very carefully, and heard Amos hold back a gasp of pain. Fargo moved the shoulder again, pressed with his fingers, probing gently. "Bad strain but nothing broken, I'd say," he concluded.

"I can tell you that's not the only place I hurt," Amos said.

"Got a few sore places myself," Fargo said. "You see your horse anywhere?"

"Back there," Amos said, gesturing to a stand of shrubby hackberries. "Bad left hind leg, pulled tendons. Take a few weeks of rest to fix."

"We'll ride back on the Ovaro, take it very slow," Fargo said, the idea sounding appealing. It took him and Amos another fifteen minutes to find the saddles but they finally began to make their way through the brush at the bottom of the slope. Amos had diagnosed his mount's injuries correctly, Fargo saw, and applied some of the oil of wintergreen to the bruised leg. The horse limped its way along behind them, able to move without rider or saddle. The night had begun to descend when they came in sight of the herd. Robin and some of the others rushed forward and Fargo saw Eden halt her pacing, watch, a mixture of apprehension and anger in her eyes. Tom Craft had started a small cooking fire and Amos lowered himself slowly, wincing, before its warmth. He told what had happened as Fargo put the saddles away and tethered the horses. When he returned, Eden's eyes sought his at once, her face tight.

"Fifty Cree, Amos said?" she questioned. "Fifty that we saw in two groups. I'd guess there's at least that many more. A hundred or more Cree and probably that many Blackfoot. That's no damn raiding party. That's an attack force. You're saying we have to go more out of our way to find a place where we can cross the Milk and head north."

"I'm saying a hell of a lot more than that," Fargo told her. "I'm saying I'm not moving this herd anywhere until I find out what they're doing here. Something's in the wind. They're not planning any damn tea party, you can be sure of that."

"Got any ideas, Fargo?" Tom Craft asked.

"No, but it's plain that the Blackfoot have made some kind of pact with the Cree," Fargo answered.

Eden cut in and impatience held her voice. "But it's not my concern, Fargo. Getting the herd to Big Moose is all I care about."

"You can't afford to care only about that," Fargo returned calmly, and she frowned. "One thing that's always worked in the white man's favor is that the Indian tribes have always been fiercely independent. Joining forces, banding together, those are lines they just don't think along. You let the Cree and Blackfoot see what they can do together, you let them have a real victory, and you can forget this territory. You won't have a matchbox left, much less a farm, ranch or homestead."

"Maybe they're just planning to hunt together," she said.

"No," Amos said, cutting in with sudden vehemence. "First, there's no reason for 'em to do that, no reason at all."

"And second?" Fargo asked.

The parchment face seemed to grow longer, the lines pulling down across his cheekbones. "Been thinking back since we saw so many Cree are here, now," Amos said. "Don't know why it didn't hit me before. Down beside Fort Belknap, just east of Chinook, there's a big, new settlement that's gone up, maybe a hundred new homesteaders. The Blackfoot tried three times to wipe it out but the troopers at the fort stopped them each time."

Fargo stared at Amos and his brows drew together. "Damn, that's it," he breathed. "That's got to be it. That's who Jim Oddle was trying to tell us to warn. The settlers or the commanding officer at Fort Belknap." He paused, his lips drawn back.

"I'll be riding to the fort come morning," Fargo muttered. "I figure a day-and-a-half ride to reach it."

"Maybe you'll be too late by then, all of it just time wasted," Eden put in.

"No, they're still here waiting, maybe for more warriors," Fargo said. "I'll be there in time."

"And I wait here with the herd you're hired to take through. It's not fair," Eden protested.

"What's fair has nothing to do with it," Fargo said.

Her brows arched. "Then what does?"

"What's right," he snapped. Her lips pressed into each other as she spun and strode away.

He gathered his things, found a place halfway up the hill, and returned back to where Amos was just bedding down, Robin nearby. He dropped to one knee beside Amos as the old man sat up and winced at the effort.

"I'm taking you and Robin to Fort Belknap with me come morning," Fargo said. "You're in no shape to ride with the herd."

"You're sure as shooting right about that. Neither's my mount," Amos said. "But you've other reasons."

Fargo felt his smile, unable to hold it back. The wisdom of too many yesterdays lay in the old man. "Yes," he admitted. "It's the chance for you and Robin to cut out and be safe. You can rest up there, latch on to a wagon train, or just go your own way when you're ready."

"No arguin' with that, either," Amos said. "It's time. We've pressed our luck far enough."

Fargo heard Robin fling off her blanket, get up, and hurry over, a long shirt acting as a nightdress. "Speak for yourself, Amos Baker," she flung out.

Amos cast her a glance of patient understanding.

"The man's right, Robin," he said calmly. "It's time for us to move on and this is the chance for it."

"You can't make us go anywhere," she flung at Fargo, eyes flashing angrily.

"He's not making us go anywhere, Robin," Amos said, the calm staying in his voice. "It's just the time for it."

"I'll decide when it's time," she said, turned on her heel, and stomped back to her bedroll, flung herself under the blanket, her back to the two men.

"She'll understand come morning," Amos said to Fargo. The big man rose, nodded with reservations about Amos's confidence. He climbed up the hillside to where he'd left his things, undressed, and stretched out. He had taken only a deep sigh when he heard the footsteps pulling up the hill, moving with hurried anger. Robin advanced with fists clenched, her round, pugnacious little face wreathed in a mixture of hurt and fury.

"You just want to get rid of me," she accused. "You think Miss High-toned is ready to fall your way."

"You ever going to stop bristling?" Fargo asked. "You know better than that."

She stood stiffly, suddenly dropped to her knees beside him, hurt pushing aside anger. "I want to stay with you, go wherever you go when this is over," she said.

"Your memory's not that bad," he reminded. "We talked about that and you know the answer."

Her lips pushed out in a half pout and she leaned forward, her arms circling his neck, her mouth reaching up to press his lips with harsh softness. "Then one more time," she said, pulling back.

"Not if you're fooling yourself," he said.

"What's that mean?" She frowned.

"It won't change anything," he told her.

He caught the fraction of a pause before she answered. "I don't care. I just want one more time," she said, pressing herself into him.

He smiled inwardly and it was a rueful smile. It was always the same. He'd seen it often enough. They always believed him but the hoping never stopped. He drew a sigh from inside himself. She'd learn, as the others had learned. Meanwhile, one more time never hurt anyone. His hand reached up inside the long shirt she wore, closed around one round breast, and he lay back on the bedroll, Robin atop him at once as he caressed the rounded mounds. All the pugnacious aggressiveness of her lovemaking exploded into new heights, fueled by more than she wanted to understand. One more time became an explosion of panting, pumping passion almost instantly as her chunky little body seemed to virtually explode with desire. He put aside thoughts of anything else and closed the world around them.

One more time. One more moaned scream of ecstasy. One more moment never to be duplicated anywhere, anyplace, anytime.

6

The morning seemed to drag on, the afternoon, likewise, but Fargo held to the slow pace as Amos, on the extra horse, nursed his own, limping mount along. Robin rode mostly in silence, still wrestling with the disappointment she could no longer avoid as morning came and she had to realize the inner hoping was over. Just as he had told her, one more time had changed nothing.

Fargo was content with her silence as his eyes roamed ceaselessly back and forth across the terrain, memorizing markings, watching, alert for any sign of the Cree or the Blackfoot. Not that he expected any. He had swung south, away from the winding course of the Milk, skirted the base of Bearpaw Mountain, and turned north again only when he felt he was near Chinook.

By midafternoon, as he came into sight of the river, he knew he had passed Chinook and was nearing Fort Belknap. The banks of the river thinned to a single line of trees on each bank now and he glimpsed a few cabins. Only a half dozen were visible when he came into sight of the long rail fence that had been built at right angles to both banks. The other cabins and log houses that appeared were all behind the rail-fence barrier that had obviously been built as a protective line. His eyes moved along a half-dozen troopers, stationed on foot along each of the rail fences, and he halted the pinto as he saw a patrol of ten troopers move along the line of one of the rail fences. He saw them reach the distant end of the fence barrier, fan out, almost vanish as they made a long, sweeping circle and returned to hide behind the fence again.

"When was this put up?" he asked Amos as he moved the pinto forward.

"After the first attack, I heard," Amos said.

Fargo let his lips purse. "A rail fence, foot sentries, a mounted patrol, I'm surprised and impressed," he said.

"Heard the government paid most of these people to come out here and settle the land. They want 'em to stay, they have to give them protection," Amos said.

Fargo led the way to the fence and watched as one of the troopers lowered a section of split rail for the three riders to pass through. He saw more newly built log homes spreading out behind the fenced area, plenty of space between them on either side of the river, but all behind the protection of the fence and the sentries. He rode on, as Robin came up beside him, and soon he was approaching the open gate of the fort. The structure itself was modest, two wooden watchtowers over the top of the stockade and a large compound area. He saw a three-wagon train taking on supplies to one side of the compound as he halted before a sergeant, young-faced for his stripes.

"Come to see the commanding officer," Fargo said.

"Captain Riker, over there," the sergeant said and gestured to a building across the compound, a regimental flag hung outside its door.

"These folks will be staying a spell," Fargo said. "Any accommodations around here?"

"Outside, back of the fort," the sergeant said. "Dodson's rooming house, a low, white place. You can't miss it."

"Come tell us what happens when you're finished," Amos said as he turned the horse. Robin stared into the distance and remained silent. Fargo moved across the compound to the command quarters; a corporal stood guard at the door.

"Captain Riker, please," Fargo said as he swung from the Ovaro.

The corporal moved to the doorway. "Who wants him?"

"Fargo ... Skye Fargo," the Trailsman said, waited as the trooper disappeared into the office to return in a moment.

"Go on in, mister," he said, and Fargo stepped into a small office. He saw a desk, a battered file cabinet, and a territory map on the wall. Captain Riker stood behind the desk, pushing away from a worn chair, tall, young, with a military-academy cast to his face, that hint of condescension Fargo had seen on others before.

"What can I do for you, Fargo?" Captain Riker asked.

"It's the other way around," Fargo said. "I've some news for you. The Cree have crossed the border in force. They've joined up with the Blackfoot."

"The Cree? Come down from Canada? You sure of what you're saying?" Captain Riker frowned.

"Damn sure and there are others who can back

me up on it," Fargo said. He credited the captain with attentive listening as he recounted everything that had happened, step by step, from his first rescue of Robin and Amos. Captain Riker's face stayed wreathed in thought when he finished.

"Certainly a surprising development," the captain said as he frowned into space.

"Surprising?" Fargo echoed. "I'd call it a hell of a lot more than surprising. I'd call it goddamn serious."

Captain Riker's calm was irritating, his words equally so. "It could be, if you're really correct about the Cree," he said.

"I'm called the Trailsman because I know what I see," Fargo snapped.

"All right, let's agree that you're right about the Cree joining the Blackfoot," the captain conceded with unwarranted loftiness.

"That means they've got together to wipe out this whole damn settlement and maybe your fort, too," Fargo shot back.

The captain's smile was modest and deprecating. "They can't do that, of course, even if they've arranged to mount a sizable force. You saw our guardrail fences as you neared the settlement, on both sides of the river. Sentries and mounted patrols on duty day and night."

"I saw them and they're impressive enough," Fargo agreed.

"The first sign of an attack and the alarm is sounded. The full battalion turns out of the fort. There is no way they can come at us without being seen, no matter if they attack from one side or both," the captain said. "They haven't been able to surprise us since their first attempt to wipe out the settlement. They can't any longer." His face took on an expression of smugness again.

"So you figure to just sit and wait," Fargo said.

"It'll be more than enough," the captain answered. "The fact is, I don't think the Blackfoot will attack the settlement at all, even with their new Cree friends to back them up. They were badly hurt in their last two tries. They know my precautions here. They know they can't hit us by surprise any longer, and without surprise they've nothing."

The man's smugness was annoying and Fargo felt the effort of holding his temper. "Then why in hell do you think the Cree have come down in force to join them?" he questioned.

The captain shrugged. "There are a number of possibilities. They could have decided on a common migration north or they could be joining together to carve out a new, joint territory west toward Cut Bank and Alberta," he said.

"Those are both reason enough to go after them," Fargo said.

"My responsibility is to this settlement. Those are my orders, Fargo: guard these new settlers, not to go chasing down Indians. And I repeat, I doubt very much they'll be attacking us."

Fargo felt his anger snap at the man's complacency. "You doubt," he echoed. "You'll find it harder to doubt an arrow up your ass. I've said my piece." He whirled and stalked from the little office, climbed onto the pinto, and cleared the compound in a gallop. He swung around back of the fort where he saw additional homesteaders strung out in the distance. He spotted Amos seated on the front steps of the long, low-roofed, white building. He swung from the pinto to see Amos fix him with a narrowed stare.

"Didn't go well," Amos grunted, reading the set of his face. Fargo saw Robin come from the house. "He didn't believe you?" Amos probed.

"He believed me. He just thinks he's got nothing to worry about. He's convinced they can't surprise him, can't pull off a successful attack even with the Cree added."

Amos thought for a moment. "You warned him. He'll likely increase sentry patrols."

"Probably," Fargo said, then recounted the captain's remarks.

"Maybe he's right, Fargo," Amos offered. "As the man said, they've tried before. They know what's waiting for them. Maybe they are going after something else. Maybe we had it figured wrong."

Fargo's brows knitted. "Maybe," he conceded, unable to reject the possibility yet not able to accept it.

"What now?" Robin asked.

"I go back. I've said all I've got to say. There's nothing more for me to do here," Fargo answered.

Amos rose, grasped the big man's hand. "Thanks for everything, Fargo. Maybe we'll meet up again someday, someplace."

"I'd like that," Fargo answered. "Stay well, old man."

Amos turned away and Fargo saw Robin move to stand in front of him, the half pout pushing her lower lip forward, her pert face quietly pugnacious. "I'm glad for last night, even if it didn't change anything," she murmured. "And I hate you because you're going on alone."

He grinned down at her as he gathered her into his arms. She clung to him for a long moment, pulled back finally. "You'll find somebody else worth more than a half hour of your time," he told her, and she nodded but there was no conviction in her nod. She spun away and raced into the house, not looking back, and he pulled himself onto the Ovaro and rode away.

He passed the entrance to the fort, felt the grimness stab at him, and continued on. His eyes swept the new cabins that stretched along both sides of the river that passed lazily between them. He rode slowly, his gaze taking in the scene, then drew to a halt. Women washed clothes in hardwood tubs, some stacked firewood, and he watched the youngsters, lots of youngsters, most playing games, some tending to chores. The cabins stretched on into the woods; the men were mostly still clearing land around them, the scene much the same on both sides of the river. A half-dozen towheaded youngsters chasing a pig caught his attention as they shouted and laughed and ran in wild circles. He stayed, watching, and felt the terrible ominousness come over him, an echo of Robin's bad feelings magnified a thousand times. His eyes scanned the sentries by the split-rail fence and the feeling only remained, grew stronger, oppressively ominous.

"Goddamn," he swore, and sent the pinto into a gallop, suddenly wanting only to get away from the scene, the peacefulness of it, the men, the women and children, and the sentries protecting them. It suddenly all seemed a sham, a mockery, all of it cloaked with an invisible curtain of tragedy. But he could put nothing together that made the terrible ominousness more than a feeling and he sped through the opening in the fence one of the sentries made for him, continued on in a gallop until he finally reined in the horse and his own churning feelings.

He slowed as the day started to wind down,

stayed along the flatland of the riverbank. The terrible ominousness remained, like a rock in the pit of his stomach. Night dropped its black curtain on the land but the moon quickly took to the sky, a waning moon, he noted, in its last quarter. He gave it two or three nights more and then it would be gone, to reappear next as a slim crescent, hardly more than a silver pencil mark in the sky. He rode on and the long hours went slowly when he finally saw the foliage growing heavier along the riverbanks, the tree cover thickening quickly.

It was time to turn south and find the spot where he'd left the others. He had started to make his turn when he caught the movement in the trees, yanked hard at the pinto to pull the horse behind the low-hanging foliage of a sandbar willow. He held his hand to the horse's muzzle, calmed him, kept him from blowing air as he saw the riders pass within yards of him. He counted six, the moonlight strong enough to let him determine the first three as Blackfoot, the other three as Cree. He waited till they'd gone on and backed the pinto from behind the willow, moved slowly in a wide circle to avoid the six braves before cutting south.

Patrolling. The word stabbed at him. They were patrolling the riverbank as he'd seen the others do. He swore under his breath as he rode south, the frown knitting his brows together. He made a cut to his left, caught the odor of the steers, and followed his nose. But the frown was still in his brow as he came into the campsite, called out as he saw Howie raise a rifle.

"It's him," he heard the man call as he rode in and slid from the saddle, sank to the ground to stretch tired limbs. He glanced up to see Eden moving out of the shadows toward him. The coffeepot still rested on the few glowing embers of the cooking fire and he poured himself a tin cup of the hot brew, drank it down eagerly, felt its strength curl inside him. Eden halted and he let her wait, knew the questions that hung on her tongue and suddenly knew that the answer he'd returned with was no answer at all. He stared at the coffee in the tin cup, the frown heavy on his forehead.

Finally she could wait no longer. "Did your good deed?" she said, unable to keep the tartness from her voice.

"Tried," he grunted.

"What does that mean?" she questioned quickly.

He clipped the words at her, told her of Captain Riker's complacency, the man's smug certainty that he had the settlement fully protected. Eden's reply carried the sharp edge of controlled anger in its sarcasm. "It would be amusing if it hadn't cost me so much time and delay," she stated, and his eyes grew narrow. "All this rushing down to warn of an attack and it turned out quite unneeded," she went on. "Unneeded and quite wrong."

"*No!*" He flung the word at her with sudden vehemence. "Something's wrong, goddammit."

"I'll say it again. You're a stubborn man, Fargo," Eden answered, her tone a dismissal.

"I ran into another patrol near the river just north of us, the same place I saw the others," Fargo blazed back. "Cree and Blackfoot. Why are they patrolling this part of the river so heavily? Why is this part of the river so goddamn important to them?"

She shrugged. "It's where they're crossing. They don't want anyone else to see them."

He shook his head doggedly, his fingers tight around the handle of the tin cup. "Something more, goddammit, something more," he growled. "I'm going to find out come tomorrow night. There'll be enough moon left. Goddamn, I'm going to find out once and for all."

Eden's eyes caught pale blue fire. "I'm not wasting another twenty-four hours while you keep on chasing down that wild imagination of yours," she flung at him.

He rose, emptied the coffee grounds in the tin cup over the few remaining embers, and fastened Eden with a steel-blue stare. "I'm tired and bothered and I'm only going to say this once," he began. "You can look at it this way. I saved your ass twice. You owe me, your own words. All right, I'm collecting. I'm going to do what I have to do and I don't want any more lip from you, honey."

He watched her eyes, saw his words had touched her sense of fairness despite her anger. She turned away from him and strode off without another remark, still maintaining her controlled, tight-assed little walk. He took his things behind a wild cherry bush and was asleep in minutes. The night sounds were the usual ones and he slept undisturbed until the day swept the night away. He woke, washed at the small stream, and walked down to the campsite. The men were taking coffee and johnnycakes; they watched him draw near. He knew they expected answers. They deserved as much and they listened to him in respectful silence. He finished by telling them he wanted another twenty-four hours wait before moving on.

"That's fine with me," Tom Craft said. "I'm in no hurry, especially to tangle with a forestful of Cree and Blackfoot."

Fargo saw Eden come up, clothed in the gray shirt and the gray riding skirt that gave her pale blue orbs a gray tone. "You can move the herd whenever you're ready," he said, and saw the surprise widen her eyes. "Back and forth, a few miles each way. It'll let them stretch and keep them calm when the night comes," he said.

"Of course," she snapped. "I thought you'd come to your senses for a moment. Or decided to do the job you were hired to do."

He studied her. "Maybe Robin was right about you," he said as he walked from her.

"Right about what?" he heard her call. "Damn you, explain that."

He halted as she strode up to him. "Once a bitch always a bitch," he said. "That explain it enough?" Her hand flew to the quirt at her waist, halted as she read the warning in his eyes.

"You believe that?" she asked and he suddenly saw something touch the pale blue orbs, a flash of hurt.

"You make it damn hard not to," he said. Her lips tightened and she turned, strode away. He watched her go. She continued to remain a contradiction, he thought. Maybe as much to herself as anyone else. He walked on to where the Ovaro grazed, sat down and watched Eden and the men start to move the herd. He lay back but the tension inside him refused to let him relax and he filled a few hours by currying the pinto. But the day continued to move with agonizing slowness, and to help kill time he helped bring the steers back as the afternoon finally wore on.

He was standing alone, eyes northward, as the sun slipped behind the mountains. He welcomed the night when it finally lowered itself across the land. He let the dark deepen, his eyes following the moon as it started its climb across the sky. The waning crescent would afford just enough light, he mused, and then walked to the pinto, swung into the saddle, and turned the horse north. He started from the campsite and saw Eden watching him, her tall, willowy form barely outlined by the moon. She was still standing, watching as he disappeared into the night.

He rode directly north, stayed on the pinto across the rise and fall of the low hills that began to flatten as he drew closer to the river. He slowed, finally came to a halt when he caught sight of the first sandbar willow. He slid from the saddle, led the pinto another fifty yards on foot when he froze, the big Colt in his hand as he heard the sound of a horse coming up behind him. The oath stayed inside himself as he turned, dropped the gun back into the holster, and watched the horse and rider appear, moving slowly through the trees.

"Goddamn," he hissed, and saw the horse reined up. He was at the animal in two long strides as the rider slid to the ground, alabaster skin a soft milk white in the moon's dim light

"You get your ass out of here," he whispered, his voice a tight rasp.

"I'm going along," she said. "I want to see for myself this time. No more secondhand stories."

"You'll get us both killed," he said.

"I'm going to see for myself," she repeated doggedly. "You've one choice. Take me or I'll follow you."

"That's no choice, that's blackmail," he hissed back.

"Make up your mind. You're wasting time. I go with you or I follow."

He stared darts at her but there was little doubt she meant it. "We get out of this alive I'm going to fan your ass for this stunt," he rasped, turned from her, and moved forward. He pulled the pinto along for a few yards more, then halted, tethered the horse beneath a willow. Eden did the same with her mount. "Start crawling," he growled as he dropped flat and began to push his way forward.

She lowered herself to the ground and began to crawl alongside him. He halted every few feet to listen, draw the air into his nostrils. The smell of hide, bear grease, and buffalo oil grew heavy in the air and he picked up the sounds of sleep from all directions. The Indians were all around them and he cast a glance at Eden. The onyx hair was invisible in the dark and the alabaster skin continued to be a pale milk white but there was more determination than fear in her eyes.

He started to crawl forward again and she moved at his side, her shoulder touching his. Suddenly his hand shot out, closed over the back of her head, and pressed her face into the wet night grass. He pushed his own face deep into the ground beside her as the Indian walked past, not more than two feet away. Fargo listened, the Indian walking softly, but the Trailsman's ears followed his movement. Fargo drew his hand from the back of Eden's head and started to crawl on again. He could hear the soft lapping of the river against the bank now, and only a row of crowberry bushes still blocked his view.

He inched forward through the bushes, Eden staying beside him, and pushed the last of the brush aside to stare out at the river. He felt the exclamation hang inside him, the frown dig into his brow. From the bank, a convex mound of branches extended out into the river. He glanced at Eden, saw the incomprehension he felt in her face. It was as though a huge army of beavers had constructed a long dam of twigs and branches that stretched some fifty yards along the river bank.

"What is it?" he heard Eden whisper. "What's it covering?"

He felt his shoulders shrug on the ground and knew only one thing. He had to find out. He started to inch past the end of the bushes when the figure rose, directly in front of him at the very edge of the long mound of branches. The Indian had been lying down where the riverbank dropped off, hidden from view at the edge of the mound of branches, but now he stood up, senses alerted, his eyes moving back and forth along the shoreline. Fargo drew back and let the bushes close in front of him. His hand reached down to the Arkansas throwing knife inside the leather sheath strapped to the calf of his leg. He drew the thin, perfectly balanced blade from the sheath, brought its double-edged deadliness up to rest for a moment on the grass as he peered through the bushes.

The Indian remained standing, eyes slowly moving along the shoreline, across the bushes and the sandbar willows that touched the water's edge. Fargo pushed himself half up with one hand pressed into the ground, drew the knife back in his upraised arm. The Indian caught the motion in the bushes at once, his brows coming together. He peered into the spot as he drew the tomahawk from his waistband, took a half step forward when Fargo fired the knife, putting every shoulder and arm muscle behind the throw. The thin blade hurtled out of the bushes, too narrow and moving too fast to see in the dark. It struck the Indian at the base of the neck, at the small V in the collarbone, moving with such force that it penetrated up to its hilt. Fargo followed the blade, then streaked from the bushes as the Blackfoot stiffened, his hands clawing at his neck. Fargo caught him as he started to fall, lowered him silently to the ground, stayed in a crouch, his eyes darting up and down the riverbank.

Nothing else moved and he beckoned to Eden. She came out of the cherry bushes as he drew the thin blade free and a small bubble of red came from the small hole. Fargo wiped the blade clean on the grass, returned it to its holster, and moved to the edge of the convex mound of branches and twigs.

With Eden's help, he began to remove the top branches, then the next layer; most still had leaves on them. A thin third layer of long twigs was last and he pulled them aside to finish opening a narrow hole. He stepped into the water that lapped lazily at the shoreline, blinked, took a moment to let his eyes adjust to the dark beneath the mound of branches. He felt the water move as Eden came in beside him and his eyes began to discern the shapes under the branches, long, graceful shapes that curved upward at each end, and his hand reached out to touch the bark of the nearest. He heard Eden gasp out the word. "Canoes."

He echoed it. "Canoes. Goddamn canoes. There must be at least fifty under these branches," he whispered, and it suddenly all fell into place and he heard the sharp intake of his own breath as the full realization hit him. His racing thoughts broke off as he heard voices. From under the mound of branches, they sounded strangely disembodied. They were still distant but growing in strength, one of the patrols moving along the bank. He turned, forced himself to move slowly and avoid splashing the water. He reached out and dragged the Blackfoot's lifeless form into the water.

"Pull those branches back in place from inside here," he hissed at Eden, and she nodded, began pulling back the twigs, then the branches, working them into place from inside the mound. Fargo pushed the Blackfoot's body underwater, held it there until it began to sink, and then helped Eden finish putting the last of the branches back, reaching out through the openings from inside. It'd do, he thought, and heard the voices again, sounding muffled from inside the mound, but they were near. He lowered himself waist-deep into the water, pulled Eden down with him. He stayed motionless as the bucks passed by outside, moved on down along the shoreline.

"They'll be back," he breathed.

"How do we get out of here?" Eden whispered.

"The way a beaver would," he breathed back, and took her arm, pushed past the first row of birchbark canoes, moved into deeper water. He pushed to the other edge of the branches with Eden. She was but a shape in the blackness but she understood the pull on her arm as he dived under the water. He felt her come with him as he swam underwater in the pitch blackness and surfaced when he was certain he'd cleared the edge of the branches that extended out into the river. Eden's head bobbed up beside him. "Float," he whispered into her ear. "Let the current take you downriver."

She nodded again and he let himself go with the slow current; only the very top of her head was above water. He saw the bucks on the shore, small knots of them asleep while others patrolled. He stayed with the current, let it carry them downriver far beyond where the Cree and Blackfoot had encamped, finally turned and swam for shore. He pulled himself up onto the bank, the water warm, the night air hot, helped Eden as she emerged close behind him. He headed away from the river, climbed a slope that became a small hill, halted high up from the Milk below, and sank down where the moon cast its waning light on a bed of pine needles.

"That's it," he said as Eden came down alongside him, her gray blouse clinging to the long line of her breasts as she lay back, drawing deep drafts of air.

"I thought we were finished," she said.

"That's it," Fargo repeated. "It all fits now, every damn piece, from why they were so hell-bent on wiping out Amos and Robin to their patrols. They're going to attack by canoe. They'll slip down the Milk without a sound, past the sentries and patrols in the blackness. They'll come out of the canoes, hundreds of them, like shadows. They'll have the whole damn settlement near wiped out before the good captain inside his fort even knows what's going on. They'll teach him how many ways surprise can come. They've been bringing the canoes down from Canada in ones and twos, to be sure nobody got suspicious of anything, then hiding them under that beaver dam they built. All they had to do was be sure nobody got near. That's why the Milk was so important to them." He paused, smashed his fist into his palm. "Stinking, rotten bastards, they planned it well and it'll work. They'll butcher every man, woman, and child in that settlement."

"What have they been waiting for? Why haven't they attacked before now?" Eden asked.

He pointed to the dim crescent now far down its

path across the sky. "There's been too much moon till now. Tomorrow night will be moonless, pitch black. Those sentries won't see or hear a thing as the canoes slip downriver, until it's too late."

"You did all you could do," she said. He rose, pulled off the wet shirt, and hung it on a branch, the anger hard in his face.

"All wasn't enough," he shot back.

"You certainly can't stop them all by yourself," Eden said. "Besides, the only thing that would stop them now would be to get rid of their canoes, and you'd have no chance of doing that alone either."

He stared at her, thoughts exploding inside him. "That's right," he said, his brow furrowing. "No canoes, no surprise. It all hangs on their slipping downriver in the canoes."

Eden frowned at him. "You're a complete fool if you're thinking you can go back there and destroy all those canoes," she said.

"No, I can't do that," he said as he felt the excitement seize his gut. "But there's a way, god-damn there's a way. I can wreck the canoes when they're loaded, destroy canoes and crews at once."

"What are you talking about?"

"The herd," he said. "We'll stampede the herd right into them when they start downriver."

He saw her eyes widen in shock. "You're insane."

"No, dammit, it'll work. It's the one thing that can work. I'll get close enough to watch them. They'll have to take off all that covering of branches, bring the canoes to the shore and get the bucks into each canoe. I'd guess five or six to a canoe. That'll all take time. We can have the herd ready. When I give the signal, we send them stampeding right across the river into the canoes."

"No," Eden bit out. "The whole thing is crazy. Besides, I came to bring that herd to Big Moose, not to lose it in a stampede."

"We'll be able to round up most of them afterward," Fargo said. "It might take a few days but we'll find them."

"Don't lie to me, Fargo. We won't ever find a damn one," she snapped, and he let his shrug admit the possibility.

"I'll have to take that chance," he said.

"You'll do nothing of the sort," she said, getting to her feet, a tall, willow shape, the wet clothes outlining the curve of her long body. "You warned the captain. You did your best."

"Dammit, Eden, it'll be a massacre if we don't stop them."

"I'm not losing my herd to do good deeds," she flung back.

His eyes became blue flint. "You're lucky I didn't feel that way when I chased after McMurtree."

"That's hitting below the belt."

"I'm going to do more than that. You don't know what it means to really feel. You've kept that fire inside you under that ice cover for too goddamn long. You don't know about crying and hurting and wanting. You kept yourself off to one side, everything at arm's length, people looked at from a distance. Well, you're going to learn another way now."

He tore at his wet Levi's, yanked them off. "What are you doing?" she blurted, fear in her pale blue eyes. He stood before her in underpants, then tore them away and knew his organ had already begun to rise in anger and wanting, two sides of the same coin. He saw Eden stare at the thickening, thrusting tool, tear her eyes away. "No," she gasped. "No."

But his hand shot out, caught the front of the wet blouse, pulled, and the buttons flew open. He spun her around as he tore the blouse from her, his eyes taking in the long breasts, full and beautifully rounded with lifting undersides. He tore the clasp open at the skirt and sent the garment sailing into the bushes. Eden's hand went to the quirt still tucked into her belt but he tore it from her, undid the belt, and flung it aside. She landed on the pine needles, long, magnificent legs, her torso molded into a small waist and hips that flowed outward in a delicate curve. She tried to twist away, turned onto her stomach, but he caught her wrist, yanked her around onto her back as he tore the last garment from her, enjoyed the sight of her naked loveliness, flat abdomen and a very curly, black nap beneath.

"Bastard," she screamed, tried to kick long, lovely legs at him but he avoided the blows, closed one hand around her ankles, and flipped her onto her stomach. He fell over her smooth rear, rose, and whirled her onto her back. He kissed her, his mouth pushing her lips aside as his tongue darted forward. "No, no, damn you," she half screamed, and he let his hand press over one long breast, the alabaster skin creamy soft. "Oh . . . oh, no," she cried but he put his mouth to the pink tip inside the dusty rose circle. "Oh . . . oh, stop," she called out but there was more submission than command in her cry. His tongue circled the dusty rose circle, nibbled its way around the nipple; he felt the tiny tip grow firm, rise. He pulled, gently, and she continued to cry out little protests but her hands had flattened against his back.

He began to move atop her, his pulsating strength resting against her lower belly, nestled in the curly, soft wire triangle. "You . . . you . . . oh, God . . . you . . ." she gasped as his mouth pulled from one breast, nibbled its way down along her rib cage. His finger pushed down across her belly, rested in the curly bush, and moved downward, found the little mound beneath it, moved lower. "Please, no, please, oh, no . . . oh, please," she murmured. His hand stayed, caressed her, moved down again to touch the damp warmth of her thighs. He lifted his hips, pushed his organ to the very tip of her soft folds, pressed ever so slightly, let it rest there. "Oh, Jesus, Jesus," she moaned, and he felt her abdomen suck in. He followed with the throbbing tip of his maleness, pushed in a fraction deeper, letting himself touch the elliptical opening. "Aiiiiii . . . oh help me . . . oh, oh . . ." sounds falling from her lips and then suddenly he felt her mouth open around his, pull, push, her tongue coming forward. Her hands moved up and down his back, small butterfly swoops.

"Bastard," she moaned. "Oh, God . . . oh," and her moistness flowed forth, warmth that pulled him in further and he felt the tension inside her vertical lips. Her long body twisted, moved in a quick upward thrust as if she suddenly had to impale herself on him, the push so sudden it took him by surprise. Her scream was high, sharp, pain and pleasure curled inside it. "Iiiiiiiii . . . oh, oh, oh," tiny little gasps as she stayed impaled around him and he felt her throbbing, loosening, flowing. She groaned, a suddenly deep sound, and her hands fell from his back, cupped her breasts, and pushed them upward to his mouth, offerings no longer withheld, offerings given with sudden, sweeping intensity. Her long body began to move up and down beneath him, drawing him deeper into her, and tiny moans came with each sinuous thrust. He fell into rhythm with her, her body transformed into serpentine wanting, the barrier destroyed, the fire set free as her alabaster skin rubbed against him, creamy soft warmth, every part of her awake with new knowing.

He rose and pushed with her, began to quicken her pace and felt her stomach suck in again. "Ah ... ah ... ah, yes, yes ... more, more," she cried, and he saw the onyx hair toss and turn against the pine-needle flooring as she seemed about to burst out of her very being. He felt the contractions begin deep inside her, felt her calves tighten, then her long thighs against him, the contractions increasing, pulsating around his own throbbing. Her scream seemed to reach the treetops as he came with her, a spiraling sob of ecstasy, more than pleasure, more than passion, the wonder of discovery in it, and he stayed with her, the inner palpitation hanging on, twitching finally, tremors of the flesh unwilling to give up ecstasy, and finally she lay beside him, her lovely, long form drawing in deeply with each breath. She would always be a contradiction, fire and ice, but now she knew the fire and she would never be the same again.

Her eyes opened slowly, the pale blue frost now a glaucous smoldering. She stared at him and he saw the whirl of thoughts behind her eyes, watched the tiny furrow come to crease the cream-white forehead.

"Maybe you expect too much too soon," she said.

"No," he answered.

She thought a long moment. "You teach well," she said.

"You're a hell of a pupil," he answered. She fell

silent and he knew she waited for his words. "I'm going to stampede the herd into those goddamn canoes," he said quietly.

Her rounded, lovely shoulders lifted. "I can't say yes," she said. "But I can't say no anymore either."

"That's good enough for now. Learning takes time."

She turned to him, raised one long, willowy leg, drew it over his thigh. "Is there time for another lesson?" she breathed.

His eyes flicked to the mountains. The dawn hadn't edged its way over their ridged beauty yet. "Time enough," he said as he pressed his mouth around one alabaster-skinned breast. He thought, for a fleeting moment, of what lay ahead, and wondered if it might be the last lesson for pupil and teacher. He drew the sweet mound deep into his mouth. He'd make it a lesson to remember for a day or a lifetime.

7

She'd fallen asleep on top of him and he woke her as the dawn pink began to edge the mountains. He pressed his hand into the alabaster, firmly soft rear and she opened her eyes, sat up, stretched. He found himself yearning to stay there all day and drink in her long, supple beauty. "What are you thinking?" she asked as she leaned back, her long, full-bottomed breasts curving upward.

"I was thinking I've something in common with Adam, now," he said, and her eyes questioned. "I know what it's like to be in Eden," he said, tossed her a slow smile.

She sat up, came to him, rubbed her breasts against his chest. "Adam was expelled. You won't be," she murmured.

"I'll remember that," he said as he pulled himself to his feet. She reached out before he could draw on shorts, curled her fingers around him, drew him against her cheek as she leaned against his powerful thigh.

"So much more to learn, isn't there?" she murmured through half-closed lips as she held him to her.

"All in time," he said as he lifted her to her feet.

He dressed quickly, watched her slip into the gray shirt and gray skirt, add the belt and the quirt and become coolly contained at once, the transformation startling if not magical. But her eyes couldn't find the frost that had always held there; they were softer, now. She'd never find it again, except in anger, he knew, and he led the way down the slope on foot as the new day began to take possession of the land. He stayed away from the river, Eden hurrying with him, her hand in his, until he had to turn north to retrieve the horses. The grass grew high as he neared the land behind the riverbank, and he moved forward in a crouch, pulling her down with him.

"What if they found the one you killed?" Eden asked.

"No chance. He won't surface for days," Fargo said. He spotted the tree, veered left a few degrees, stayed down until he had ducked into its long, hanging, pendantlike branches. He untied the horses, swung onto the pinto, and waited for Eden to take her saddle. He sent the pinto flying out of the willow in a full gallop and Eden followed, caught up to him.

"Did you see them? Are they coming for us?" she asked, alarm in her voice.

"No, just playing safe, getting the hell out of here," he said, and slowed when he had put enough distance behind him. The men were just taking coffee when he rode into the campsite with Eden and he saw the questions waiting in their eyes. He slid from the saddle, took a cup of the hot coffee Howie held out to him as Tom Craft brought a cup to Eden.

"I found answers, not the kind I wanted to find," Fargo began. He painted the picture in short, terse sentences, leaving out nothing. There was no need to dramatize; the truth was more than enough. Eden lifted her voice as he finished telling the men how the Cree and the Blackfoot had planned their moves.

"Fargo thinks there's one way to stop the massacre," she said. "Stampede the herd into the canoes as they start downriver."

Rob Boyson's eyes duplicated the astonishment in all the other men's stares. "You serious?" he asked the big man with the lake-blue eyes.

"All the way," Fargo answered. "There's no other way to stop them. If they get downriver in those canoes, it's all over for every soul in that settlement."

"But stampeding the herd into 'em, Jesus," Tom Craft muttered, awe flooding his voice.

"It'll be tricky and it'll take timing and a lot of luck, but it can work. It's the only thing that can," Fargo said.

Eden's voice cut in. "I told him to go ahead," she said with quiet firmness. "Maybe it means sacrificing the herd and maybe we can salvage it afterward. I don't know. I can't say I don't care. But if it comes down to cows or kids, a herd or a homestead, I guess there's not much choosing to do." She paused, swept the men with her steady, sober stare. "It won't be a picnic. Any man who wants to cut out now can do so and I'll understand. Full pay no matter what you decide. Talk it over among yourselves."

She turned away, walked to one side, and Fargo went with her. "Surprised?" she murmured, and looked pleased with herself.

"Some," he said. "And maybe a little proud of you." She pressed his arm against her and looked more than pleased. The men had moved back to draw themselves into a small circle, their voices low, and Fargo waited beside Eden until he saw them turn, walk toward them. Rob Boyson focused on the big man, his question the one plainly in all their minds.

"You really think it can work, Fargo?" he asked.

"If it goes right, it'll finish most of them. No canoes, no surprise, and nobody left for any massacre," he said. "There'll be enough left to go after us but not that many, I hope."

The men exchanged another glance among themselves and Tom Craft spoke up first. "Count me in," he said. "I can't see pulling out when we can stop a massacre."

"That's worth fighting for any day," one of the others said.

"Wouldn't be able to sleep much if I didn't try," another said, and Fargo saw the agreement was complete.

"Then it's settled." As Tom Craft poured more coffee, Fargo sat down on the ground and laid out the plans that had been only loosely formed inside himself. They took shape, form, reality as he outlined them.

"There'll be no trouble stampeding the herd," Rob Boyson said. "They're real edgy. Too much standing around."

"Good," Fargo said. "We'll move them into place before the morning ends, let them stand there and get edgier."

"One thing," Tom put forth. "You're going to watch the Indians, wait for them to start downriver. When we hear your shot we send the herd into a stampede. We'll shoot on both sides of them and they'll take off. But the Cree and the Blackfoot will hear the shots."

"They'll hear, all right, but the shots will be plenty far back at first. I'm betting they'll take it as nothing to do with them. If anything, they'll speed up moving downriver," Fargo answered.

"Good enough."

"Now let's move the herd." Fargo led the way to a spot some two miles downriver from where the Cree and Blackfoot had assembled. He moved the herd into position, went over the plans another half-dozen times. "I'll take a dry run," he said, mounted the pinto, and sent the horse racing toward the river at the full gallop of a stampeding herd. He made the run twice and there were but a few seconds' difference between the two.

"All right," he said, drawing a long breath as he squatted down with the others. "The stampeding herd will reach the river in just under two minutes. They'll keep going, crashing right into the river. They won't stop. I'll add another half minute for me to fire the first shot and you to start them off, another half minute for the herd to get into full stampede. That's three minutes in all. That's what we have to work with, three minutes. It'll work, I'm sure of it."

"Nothing more to do but wait, now," Rob Boyson said.

"You all know what you have to do in those three minutes. Lay down, rest, take it easy till then," Fargo said, and the men drifted back to the rear of the herd. Fargo walked on and Eden fell into step beside him as he climbed up onto a hillside.

"You forgot something," she said, asperity in her voice. "You told each of the men what they have to do. You made your dry run. You know what you're going to do. Where do I fit in?"

He sat down, drew her to the ground beside him, a curtain of low-hanging branches in front of them. "Backup. Stand-in. Insurance," he said. "Call it whatever you like. You'll wait at the bank. Anything can happen. I could make a mistake. They could catch me, put a dozen arrows through me. You'll wait at the bank. If I haven't fired that first signal shot by the time those canoes reach you, you fire it. That's all that will count, then, the signal to set that stampede going. If I can't do it, it'll be up to you."

She lay back against him, her face grave, stayed silent for a long while. When she spoke, her words were pulled out of her own thoughts. "They'll never know."

"Who'll never know?"

"If you do it, if you pull it off, they'll never know at the settlement," she said. "It doesn't seem right."

"I don't need any medals," Fargo said. "It's that way more often than not in life. Things we don't know about decide whether we live or die, laugh or cry. Sometimes it's best that way."

"It's best knowing," she disagreed, and he saw the tiny smile touch her lips. She came against him, arms encircling his neck. There was but a half hour before dusk, he guessed, and wished it could be different but the grayness had already begun to slide over the high ridges. He held her awhile longer, then pulled her to her feet with him. He stepped from the curtain of branches and his eyes moved back to the south. The herd was close enough, yet beyond sight, and he grunted in satisfaction as he turned down the hillside and moved toward the river, leading the pinto on foot, Eden beside him with her own mount. He found a thick hawthorn and put her horse beneath it, brought her to the edge of the river.

"Stay here," he said. "You'll be able to see upriver from here, but it'll be damn dark. You won't see the canoes till they're almost at you. You'll do better using your nose."

She nodded. "And if I hear your signal shot?"

"Hit the saddle and get off to the side, because those steers are going to charge right through here." He started to pull himself onto the pinto when her arms came around him, her lips warm sweetness on his, her breasts soft cushions against his chest.

"For yesterday and for tomorrow," she said, and stepped back. He climbed onto the pinto and turned the horse west along the bank of the Milk River. The Indians had come across the border on its lazy current. They planned to make it their avenue for murder and massacre. It was only fitting that the river become their grave. He quickened his pace as the purple gray of dusk tinted the shore, followed the bank as it made a slow curve, and reined in as he saw the trees thicken. He swung from the horse, moved forward on foot, leading the pinto behind him until he guided the horse beneath a thicket of sandbar willows, tethered the horse to one of the drooping branches. In his long, loping stride, he moved forward again, staying at the edge of the trees that came down almost to the very water. The half-light was still with him as he came into sight of the long cover of branches where it jutted out into the river. He dropped to one knee, peered forward. The warriors had pulled back on their patrols and as he watched, near-naked bucks began to carefully pull the branches and long twigs from the elaborate beaver-dam cover.

They worked carefully, slowly, taking precautions not to puncture the birchbark canoes with a sharp length of branch. He counted at least sixty pulling apart the branches, saw that many more gathering along the bank. One figure moved back and forth, apart from the others, barking directions in short grunted words. The figure turned and Fargo saw the large-nosed Cree that had led the chase after him up into the rocks. The Indian's golden-eagle feather rose at an angle from a thin, rawhide headband and Fargo saw something else. The Cree wore war paint, broad white and dark red streaks that ran down his face. Fargo's glance went to the others waiting in the trees and the brush and caught the painted colors on each face. He risked pushing a dozen yards closer as the light began to fade, made his way along the treeline in quick, darting movements. Halting, he watched a line of braves begin to pull the canoes alongside the riverbank and stayed waiting, on one knee, counting off minutes.

He had come to watch for any last-minute changes, any switch in their plans, and to be certain that this was, in fact, the night they would strike. He had guessed right but he could draw little satisfaction from that. Time was everything now. He had to wait, see them in the canoes, ready to move downriver, before he turned back. He estimated it would take them fifteen or so minutes to reach the spot where he was to fire the signal shot, another two minutes to reach where Eden waited. The bank of trees moved and Fargo's eyes stayed at the spot as the line of braves began to emerge, climb into the canoes that now stretched along the bank. More Cree than Blackfoot, he took note, easily two to one. They entered the canoes, four to six in each, just as he'd guessed. The big-nosed Cree with the golden-eagle feather halted beside the first canoe, his eyes raised upward as he watched the last flicker of the day fade away. He'd wait a little longer before stepping into the canoe, Fargo was certain, just long enough to let the night deepen.

The Trailsman rose to his feet as the darkness closed down around him. The Blackfoot and their Cree allies were moving precisely as he'd guessed they would. It was time to slip back through the night, be in place and ready to fire the signal shot when they glided silently downriver. He turned, moved into the long, loping stride that devoured time and distance. He stayed at the very edge of the bank, his feet touching the water that lapped gently at the shoreline. He could make better time there in the darkness and he bore down, increased the length of the loping stride.

He was satisfied, everything was going according to schedule, and he'd just rounded the long, slow curve in the river when he felt the bank slide out from under him. He tried to twist his body inland but the bank had become instant mud, sweeping both his feet with it and he hit the slippery soil on his back, felt his feet and legs go into the water, and then the sudden sharp bite of pain at his right ankle. He clawed at the bank with his hands, managed to halt his slide but he was already half in the river and his right foot jammed into something that hurt when he pulled back. He pulled himself up to a sitting position, reached down into the inky water, his hand moving along his right leg to his ankle. He felt the hard yet slimy, twisting mass into which his foot had jammed and he cursed in silence, an old, underground piece of tree root, long buried under the riverbank. He tried twisting his foot, turning his leg, but the root only seemed to tighten.

He felt the stab of helpless rage and his eyes peered back upriver and his ears strained to catch the soft sound of paddles in the water. But there was only silence and he tried to pull his foot free again and was rewarded only by pain. He reached down his leg again, drew the double-bladed, thin throwing knife from its sheath around his calf. Working in the blackness, his hands reaching down into the water, his position awkward and unwieldy, he began to cut at the root with the knife. But the root was a tentacle now, slippery with decades of mold and hardened into a fibrous mass. The knife kept slipping, even after he managed to make a small cut. "Goddamn," he hissed through gritted teeth and forced himself to work slowly, cut into the tentacle with small strokes. Speed and too much pressure only made the knife slip against the slime and mold that encrusted the root.

There was no way to see progress, only the feel of the knife into the small cut he'd been able to make. The seconds sounded like rifle shots inside him as they ticked away. He kept his eyes trained upriver, peering into the inky blackness as he cut into the root. He paused, his hand and wrist aching, felt the depth of the cut with groping fingers. He had made some progress, and he took the point of the knife now and used it as a small pick, pressing it into the cut. He could feel it going down deeper.

Then he heard them; first, the sound almost beyond hearing, a soft, purling sound that would have gone unheard by most men. The canoes were still out of sight in the dark of the moonless night, and in silent rage, he jammed the knife blade into the root with all his strength, plunging it into the center of the small cut. He felt the fibrous tentacle suddenly give, its core breached, the weight of it tearing away the other half, and his ankle came free. He pulled himself up onto the bank on his back, stayed motionless for a moment, eyes straining upriver, and saw the dark shapes appearing, silent wraiths, shadows on shadows.

He scooted backward further up on the bank, swung himself, leaped to his feet in a crouch, landing on his toes. With another quick glance at the dark shapes in midriver, he began to run again, staying in the crouch, the loping stride carrying him with almost lupine effortlessness. He streaked through the black night, painfully aware that the canoes were gliding with equal swiftness through the water. He had to stay ahead of them, far enough ahead to reach the pinto and outdistance them. His eyes flicked to the trees lining the shore as he ran and he felt the tightness beginning to pull inside his chest.

He slowed, peered forward at the trees, and saw the pendant shape of the thicket of sandbar willows. He half ran, half stumbled to the trees and the pinto whinnied at once. Fargo rested his head against the saddle for a moment, pulled himself onto the horse, and moved from inside the thicket. He guided the pinto to the soft soil of the riverbank that muffled hoofbeats, sent the horse into a trot, let himself gather a little more space, and broke into a full gallop. Even so, time had been more than cut in half. They were moving swiftly behind him, he knew. They had no need to paddle silently yet. He raced the pinto forward, saw the cutback in the trees that marked the spot where he'd fire the signal shot. His feet touched the ground before the pinto came to a halt and he dropped to one knee, the big Colt in his hand already. His eyes peered upriver, straining, and the shadowed shapes materialized. He waited, ticked off seconds, remembered the time he had figured for the herd to reach the river.

He raised the Colt and fired, a single shot that split the stillness. It took only seconds when he heard the exploding volley of shots in the distance and he stayed on one knee, watched as the first of the long line of canoes began to glide past him. The distant shooting continued, began to grow louder. The men were racing behind the herd and along the sides, he knew, and the shooting stopped. There was no need to waste bullets. The herd was in full stampede by now. Fargo's eyes stayed on the river. The canoes were moving two and three abreast downriver now. They'd go into silent single file when they reached the settlement, of course, and his lips drew back. He felt both fear and confidence pulling at him. Suddenly he heard the sound, a fast-growing rumble, as though it were distant thunder, and then the very ground began to tremble. The distant thunder grew stronger, a suddenly overwhelming sound. He moved the pinto forward, cast a glance at the river. The lead canoes were just passing. He peered across the night and saw the giant black mass come into view, channeled into raging, blind fear, the riders behind and on each side falling back. The stampeding herd became a thundering roar, shaking ground, trees, the very air.

His eyes went to the river. The Indians saw the hurtling mass of steers now, started to turn, but they piled into each other, those coming up in the rear unable to halt in time. They were paddling furiously, backing and turning, as the herd hit the river, their tremendous surging momentum sending them onward over the long, shallow bank. Fargo watched as the stampeding cattle hurtled into the canoes, even those in deep water being pushed forward. He saw figures being tossed into the air, the sound of birchbark being crushed, and the gargled screams of men being trampled into the river by the surging, wild mass, a hundred thousand pounds of insensate force. The night filled with screams, pain-filled cries, gurgling sounds, and he saw two Cree hurtled skyward almost in front of him as their canoe disappeared beneath the huge, crushing bodies of the steers. More than half the herd had reached the other bank and the others, still in mindless flight, spread out as they hit the river. The canoes that had managed to escape the first crushing mass found themselves smashed by smaller clusters of hurtling steers.

Fargo pulled the pinto back as the last of the steers piled into the river, still in headlong flight and, through the dust, he saw the slender form atop the horse that galloped toward him.

She reined up beside him and he saw the shock and awe in her face. "My God," she breathed. "It was horrible. I'll never be able to forget it, never."

His eyes went to the river and there was suddenly almost silence, a cry of agony that ended in a gurgling rattle, a distant moan and the roiled waters slapping hard against the bank. "They came to massacre. They found one, a different kind," he said.

The men came up, singly and in pairs and their eyes, too, held shock. "How many do you think got away?" Tom Craft answered.

"Not a hell of a lot," Fargo answered. "There

were some two hundred. I'd guess not more than twenty-five made it."

"They'll be in no condition to fight," someone else remarked.

Fargo swung from the pinto. "It's only a few hours till morning. We'll cross by day. Bed down wherever you want." Eden dismounted, followed him deep into the trees alongside the river. She lay against him as he settled onto his bedroll, content to just cling to him until she finally fell into a trembling sleep. He slept alongside her and woke with the first pink-gray light that made its way through the trees. He rose, stepped out to the riverbank, and Eden was beside him at once.

The banks of the Milk River were littered with broken pieces of canoe, bows, and arrows that drifted lazily along against the shore. He saw at least twelve dead Cree, some who'd managed to crawl up on the shore, some floating facedown in the water. A lot more lay at the bottom of the river and others had been carried downstream by the slow-moving current. His eyes went to the opposite bank, saw another ten or fifteen lifeless Cree and Blackfoot. He saw six half in the water, heads crushed, bodies caved in. Eden turned away, put her head against his shoulder. He saw the men come up to take in the detritus of bone and flesh and birchbark.

"Let's cross," he said quietly. "We've a lot of cattle to round up."

The men followed him as he led the way with Eden riding at his side. They crossed silently, the very air somehow still filled with an awesomeness, still hanging heavy with the specter of crushing, hurtling death. Once on the other bank, Fargo pushed through the trees to find a wide swath of grass that led directly north. "Start looking," he said. "Bring them onto this path. I'll meet you maybe a mile or so on." He saw Eden's eyes question. "Something I want to check out myself."

He turned the pinto as she rode off with the men and he pushed his way back through the trees to the bank. Slowly he moved the horse along the bank, his eyes scanning the shoreline. He'd ridden perhaps a half mile when he saw the canoe, intact, pulled up onto the bank. He rode to it, halted to see the footprints that led from it through the trees and out on the other side. Five sets of footprints, he noted, and his mouth drew in grimly. He'd thought the lead canoe had gone through before the herd smashed into the river. Now he was certain. He pushed the pinto forward slowly, followed the prints that led onto the grass, curved into brush. They grew very difficult to see and he noted that two took a different direction into the brush. He halted, his brow creased, and then he turned the pinto around and rode back the way he'd come.

He rode onto the wide path of grass and followed it, had gone a little more than a mile when he halted. Tom Craft, Eden, and one of the other men waited beside six steers. "Rob and the others are bringing in two more," Eden said. "They're scattered plenty far. We only caught sight of these few."

"I'll stay here with these. You go out again. It'll take time but you'll find them." He dismounted, moved to a low tree alongside the wide path, and sat down, his back against the trunk. Boyson returned with the other two steers and rode off again. Fargo watched the small knot of cattle. They were quiet, exhausted. They'd run half a week's energy

169

off in the last six hours. They'd be no problem, not for days. He sat back, waited, and it was almost dusk when Eden and the others appeared, only two more steers in tow. But Tom Craft had two jackrabbits he'd shot and he set to skinning and cooking them at once as the night lowered.

It was after they'd enjoyed the meal and the men began to bed down that Fargo saw Eden stroll to his side as he took his bedroll in hand. Her eyes studied him for a moment. "Where'd you go this morning, when the rest of us went out rounding up steers?"

"Nosing around some," he said.

"Why? What are you holding back?"

"Maybe nothing."

"Dammit, why can't you give me a proper answer?"

"Got my reasons," he said affably. "Now are you coming with me to enjoy the night or are you going to stand there and simmer?"

"You're infuriating," she snapped. "You don't deserve to enjoy the night."

He shrugged, turned, and walked away. He found a spot deep in the woods, had laid out his bedroll when she appeared, her fingers unbuttoning her shirt. "Thought you said I didn't deserve to enjoy the night," he commented blandly.

"You don't," she said. "But I do."

She came down beside him, naked in a matter of moments. He lay on the bedroll, eyes narrowed as she pressed her long, lovely body against him. There was time, he told himself, for at least one. They'd be cautious, wait, give everyone time to fall into a heavy sleep. Urgency pushed at him and he felt himself grow hard at once, push against Eden's legs as she lay half atop him. Her hand came down, found him, and she stroked, caressed, moved her body down, drew him against her cheeks, cradled, touched, uttered little gasping sounds of newfound pleasure. She wanted and yet she hesitated, unsure, the newness its own barrier, the wanting almost overwhelming.

"Oh, God, Fargo ... nice, oh, how nice ... oh, God," she murmured, rubbed against him, and he heard her breath in quick little puffs. His hand reached down, gently pressed her lips open, brought her face around. Her mouth worked, tongue darting, and he gave her the gift she wanted to take and her breath drew in, a half moan, and her lips closed around him at once and the little sounds of delight slipped through her kisses, her gentle pullings, her newfound pleasures, and he cradled her head against his stomach, let her enjoy, experiment, play, immerse herself in her wanting. When he gently tried to bring her face up, she would have none of it, tightened around him as a child clings to a new toy until finally she pulled back, lay against him, and drew in deep breaths. "Oh, Jesus, nice ... oh now nice," she murmured.

He lay her back gently, his hand cupping her soft wire nap, moving down to find she flowed in wanting, pleading. He slid into her slowly and she groaned, welcomed, and he thrust forward with sudden strength. "Aaaah ... iiiiieeee ..." she screamed, and he thrust again, harder, quicker, the sense of urgency pushing at him again. He rode her with the kind of gentle fury that quickly brought her legs up to grasp him. His mouth closed around one lovely breast and his face pressed deep into its softness. He felt her arms moving against the edge of the bedroll, flailing out, coming in to clasp him again, and then the quivering came, at

171

the back of her thighs first, then the tightening inside, shuddering little graspings of the inner flesh until she screamed in the explosion that was at once too much and too little.

When he finally drew away from her, she fell beside him, her breath shallow, almost hard. She turned, came against him, and was asleep in seconds. Fargo lay still, let his own inner throbbing subside, and closed his eyes, but not in sleep. It was perhaps fifteen minutes, he guessed silently, maybe twenty, when he heard the brush move, the footsteps stealthy through the trees. He lay as in a deep sleep as he let his ears count, one, two, three, and then two more from the rear, at his back.

Fargo's hand crept to the side to close around the big Colt he'd placed at the edge of the bedroll. His hand felt only grass. He let his fingers creep further. More grass, a small pebble, and nothing else. The gun wasn't there. Shit, he swore silently. *Goddamn shit!* He let his eyes open a fraction as he heard the footsteps moving toward the back of his head. Eden stirred, turned away, gave him an inch more room. Through slitted eyes, he saw the tall figure standing a few paces away from him, the single feather rising up into the air. The footsteps near Fargo's head had halted, the Indian inches away. Fargo saw the Cree in front of him lift his arm, point at him. Pressing palms into the ground, Fargo sprang, rolled sideways and felt the swishing sound of the tomahawk as it whistled past him to plunge into his bedroll.

Eden sprang awake with a scream and Fargo saw the Indian start to pull the tomahawk from the ground. He kicked out, caught the man in the side of the ribs and the Indian grunted in pain, fell to one knee. Fargo's fist slammed into the man's face from the side and he felt the Cree's jaw splinter from its hinges. He yanked the tomahawk from his hand as the Cree toppled to the ground, saw the second figure leaping at him from the trees. He brought the short-handled ax up and all but split the Cree's face in two as he struck at the diving figure. He ducked under the shower of blood and bone that flew over him, spun, started for the Cree chieftain, cast a glance at Eden as she huddled to one side in terror.

Two more forms appeared behind the big-nosed Cree, both with bone knives in their hands. He saw the Cree chieftain pull a tomahawk from his waist, start toward him as the other two spread out. Fargo moved backward, his eyes sweeping the ground, and he spied his gunbelt to the side, almost in the brush. He edged toward it just as the two Cree that had started to flank him came in. He drew his arm back, flung the tomahawk at the nearest Indian. The man ducked away easily but Fargo was diving for the gunbelt, landed beside it, yanked the Colt from the holster, and fired at the two Cree that rushed him. They collided in a drunken kind of dance as his shots blasted their stomachs open and they hung against each other for a moment, tottering as their insides spilled out. He didn't wait to see them fall as he swung the Colt around and saw the Cree chieftain racing into the trees.

He streaked after the fleeing form, heard the man running fast through the brush, a fleet shadow in the dark of the woods. Fargo stayed on his tail but the Cree ran like a deer, darting between trees, a black shadow too fleet to bring down. Fargo saw the Indian was increasing his lead, almost out of sight now. "Damn," Fargo swore aloud as he forced himself on faster. He could hear the man crashing through brush and he veered to the right, followed the sound, racing headlong after his quarry. He'd gone a dozen yards at a full run when he suddenly realized the sound had ended and he started to skid to a halt when the figure hurtled from the brush at him. Fargo raised his arm, twisted sideways, but the tomahawk came down, the sharp blade missing but the wooden handle crashing into his wrist. Fargo felt the Colt drop from his hand and skitter into the brush and he half fell, half rolled away and managed to avoid another blow. His hand closed around a rock where he landed, brought it up as the Cree started to come at him. He flung it, a short, straight-armed toss, and the rock caught the Indian on the forehead, a red gash erupting at once.

Fargo saw the Cree stagger backward, try to raise the tomahawk again, but he stumbled, fell against a tree. Fargo swung a tremendous blow at the man's jaw but the Indian ducked, drew new desperate strength, and brought the short-handled ax around in a whistling arc. Fargo dropped into a crouch as the tomahawk missed his head by less than an inch and he saw the ax crash into the tree trunk, bury itself halfway in. The Cree tried to pull it free and saw it was a useless effort. He spun, ran as Fargo threw another blow at him. "Sonofabitch," Fargo swore as he raced after the Cree, saw the Indian veer left, put on a burst of desperate speed. The woods thinned, opened. He was heading for the canoe, Fargo realized, streaked after the man, but the Cree was a runner, his legs devouring the ground in long strides. Fargo saw him disappear through the line of trees back of the riverbank, plunged through them after him.

He emerged to see the Cree had the canoe half into the river, one leg in the boat. Fargo flung himself through the air in a diving leap, crashed into the front end of the canoe, and sent it sideways. He heard part of the edge break away and bent low, both hands under the boat, and flung it up and over. He heard the Cree go backward into the water, raced around the canoe, and saw the Indian surface, start to climb ashore.

Faro lowered his shoulder to the end of the canoe, rammed it forward. It caught the Cree in the chest as he came out of the water and the man fell backward with a sharp gasp of pain. Fargo rammed the canoe forward again as the Cree surfaced. He felt the boat slam into the man's head and the bark break. He made his way around to the front of the splintered canoe, his eyes searching the water, and he saw the Cree surface again. The figure rose up from the water, dripping blood, his face bashed and gashed, features almost undistinguishable, and yet he staggered forward, slow plodding steps, long arms outstretched, hands reaching to close around his enemy's neck.

Fargo set himself, drew his arm back. His blow had all the strength of his powerful muscles in it and the added fury of desperation. It landed flush on the man's jaw and Fargo saw the Cree's head swivel sideways, heard the crack of neck vertebrae, and realized his blow had only finished what had already been started. The Cree slowly turned, fell forward as a dead tree finally falls to lie half in and half out of the water.

Fargo dropped to one knee, drew a long, hard breath, flexed his knuckles and his shoulder muscles. He hurt when he rose but he was the only one to rise. He slowly made his way back. The men had come running when they heard shots and they were clustered near the few steers, Eden, dressed, with them. She rushed forward as she saw him, put her arm around him until he reached a tree and leaned hard against it for support.

He saw concern, caring, and anger racing through her eyes. The anger won, as it would with her, he thought. "Dammit, Fargo, that's what you were waiting for, wasn't it?" she flung at him.

He nodded. "The first canoe got through. I found it. I knew he'd recognize me and come after me, first."

"Why didn't you tell me, dammit?" she said. "You'd no right not to."

"If I told you, you'd have been on edge. You'd have looked, stayed awake, done something, and they would have spotted it and held back. I wanted them to come in at me feeling confident," he said. "I was ready."

"Then how come it all blew apart?"

"My gun. I had it where all I had to do was reach it and blow them apart. But it wasn't there," he said, growing angry at once, still unable to understand why not. He saw her lips drop open, her eyes grow round, and his jaw grew tight.

"It was in my way when we were . . . busy," she said. "I kept hitting my arm against it. I pushed it away."

He stared at her and shook his head slowly. "You're a goddamn menace," he growled. "You almost made it your final fuck."

She came against him. "I'll never touch another thing, I promise," she said. "Nothing that isn't warm and wet, that is." She walked close against him as he moved to a quiet spot, sank down, and let exhaustion and her arms cradle him. It was over, the bad part of it. He looked forward to a long, slow trip to Big Moose.

Eden rested against him in the morning sun, the pale blue eyes misty and soft, fitting a woman who had just felt the warmth of the new sun and the heat of new passion.

"I still say it's not right, nobody knowing what happened," she said.

"Captain Riker will know," Fargo told her.

"How?" She frowned.

"I'll see to it. In my own way. He's smug, stiff, too much military academy in him, but he's not stupid. He'll know."

She came closer and he saw the satisfaction in her face. It would indeed be a good trip to Big Moose, he murmured inwardly.

8

The sun beat down on the commanding officer's quarters of Fort Belknap and outside, the Milk River wound its way between the new settlements on both sides. Captain Riker looked up at the thin, young cowboy who had just handed him the small package wrapped tightly in brown paper.

"Who'd you say gave you this to deliver to me?" the captain asked.

"Man named Fargo ... Skye Fargo. They call him the Trailsman, sir," the young cowboy said.

Captain Riker nodded. "Yes, we've met," he murmured. "Anything else, mister?"

"No, sir. He just told me to see that you got the package. And one thing else," he added uncomfortably.

"One thing else?" the captain echoed, and saw the uncomfortableness stay in the cowboy's face. "Go on, out with it," he said.

"He said to tell you that you were a lucky man," the cowboy blurted out. "That's all, sir."

"Thank you," the captain said, and waited as the young messenger hurried from his office. He opened the package slowly, laid the paper on the desk top, and peeled it back to stare down at the two arrows that lay there. One he recognized as Blackfoot. The other had to be Cree, the arrow from across the border, the two arrows that had joined together to be border arrows.

He held the two arrows in his hand as he went to the door and stared out across the compound. He nodded to himself. It fitted, made the other things make sense suddenly, the broken pieces of canoe that had drifted downriver, lots of pieces, and the bodies that had come down the Milk. He still couldn't put it all together, not the details, but he had enough to know, now. His lips pursed as he turned from the doorway, stared at the two arrows in his hand.

"Border arrows," he murmured. Message enough. He'd remember the man they called the Trailsman. Perhaps get to thank him one day.

LOOKING FORWARD

The following is the opening section
from the next novel in the exciting
Trailsman series from Signet:

The Trailsman #23:
THE COMSTOCK KILLERS

*The country around the fantastic Comstock lode,
in the 1860s.*

The tall broad-shouldered man with the lake-blue
eyes took in the angry young woman seated beside
him in the bounding, pitching Concord stage: raven-
colored hair, done neatly on top of her head, dark
brown eyes in a china-white face, and a soft but now
tightly lined mouth, a figure that even under the
present difficult conditions he could see was an
hourglass with full, high breasts pushing up from
the bodice of her trim brown-and-white traveling
dress.

With the sudden roll of the coach Skye Fargo's
arm and shoulder had pressed into the cushion of
those proud, provocative breasts, bringing a rush
of color into the girl's smooth cheeks.

"Forgive me, miss. Looks like our driver's having a rough time handling this heavy spring
rainfall."

"This coach line gives no thought to their passengers," said the round little man bouncing on his
seat across from Fargo and the girl. He was hold-

ing a derby hat in his lap. "Company ought to instruct the drivers that us paying passengers are humans and not cattle." He sniffed wetly, fingered the point of his chin. "I do a lot of traveling in these back-breakers, and let me tell you folks, a drummer's life is more thorn than rose."

The small middle-aged woman seated beside him, who was trying to hold on to anything she could— except her fellow passenger—turned her sharp nose only far enough toward the drummer to look down it, disdaining a response.

All this brought a sting of amusement to Fargo's eyes as the lurching stage once again pushed him against the lovely black-haired girl. Reluctantly he drew back, offering a further apology, though his heart was nowhere in it. The girl flicked her brown, almond-shaped eyes at the ruggedly handsome man, but now the color of her cheeks was a deep red.

"Perhaps some of the passengers need instruction too," she said icily in response to the drummer's remark. "On how to sit in their own seat!"

Skye Fargo's face split into a big grin at that. His eyes shone as he took in the angry tilt of her head, the concave line of her profile, the tip of her earlobe showing delightfully from beneath the mass of glinting black hair.

"I'm game to take some lessons," he allowed amiably. "Just haven't come across the right teacher—at least not yet."

And at that moment the coach seemed to crash into a small chasm in the road and the girl was flung almost into the big man's lap. Her hair brushed his face and for a fleeting second her hand fell against his leg, momentarily touching the bulge in his trousers.

She regained her balance, biting her lip, furiously flushed, keeping her eyes averted and not saying anything.

Fargo's attention dropped to the line of her taut bosom and he realized how really angry she was, saw it in the catch of her breathing. "Pleased to make your acquaintance," he said amiably. And he grinned as she moved elaborately away from him. "Looks like we might be getting close," he went on, lowering the coach window and putting his head out. "It's pretty much stopped raining; just some sprinkles."

"Hyah! Hyah!" came from the driver up on the box. The long black-snake whip cracked out, axles creaked, the sweating horses lunged as they raced into the canyon, while the harsh spring wind swept a sudden sheet of hard rain against the stage.

Fargo drew back inside the coach, wiping his face. He was quick enough to catch the girl smothering a laugh.

"Bit damp out there," he said with a friendly grin. "I'm happy to change your mood."

She stared coldly at him.

The drummer put the derby hat on his head, straightened it with the tips of his fingers, touched the spectacles that showed slightly from the breast pocket of his black broadcloth coat. His sharp eyes pointed at the big man seated across from him. "Your name's Fargo, I heard back at Antelope. They call you the Trailsman."

But Fargo had moved again to the window and was leaning out, the expression on his face sour.

He had a distinct feeling that something was out of balance, the kind of feeling he knew well on the trail, and which he always trusted. He didn't like the drummer recognizing him. Yet it wasn't just the fact of recognition; he'd been recognized before in his travels. It was something else about the drummer.

Had his feeling anything to do with his visiting Virginia City? He was going there in answer to a man named Conrad Rivers, owner of the Six-Mile Mining Company, who had promised him an assignment guaranteeing adventure and good money. A man couldn't ask for much more, if you threw in a girl or two.

At the same time, he was also interested in the chance of picking up any news of the remaining two of the three men who had murdered his father and mother and younger brother. The search that ran like a red thread through all the minutes of his life, the search that began when he was eighteen and had taken the name Fargo so the killers would not know him until it was too late to escape justice. The vow he had taken that nothing was ever going to stop him. He already had accounted for one of the three; it was only a matter of time till he found the other two.

The stage had now reached the top of a long, low grade and, pausing for only a moment, started down the other side at full gallop, the driver evidently intent on making good ground over the road ahead. The Concord careened into the valley, the horses scrambling and the huge wheels throwing mud and water. The momentum of the wild descent carried the horses at a gallop halfway up the next slope.

A pencil of brilliant sunlight bore down through churning, slate-colored clouds as the iron tires of the coach rang noisily against the rocky road. Again the poor footing and heavy drag of the coach slowed them to a walk. Leaning out of the window, Fargo looked up at the guard seated on the box beside the driver, saw that he had a blanket over his head to keep off the rain, though it had just stopped. The driver, in a plainsman's leather jacket, indeed looked like he was made of leather himself. He seemed to ignore the weather. His whip cracked continually and he was working himself and his horses for all he had, evidently in an effort to make up time. His head was bare, his shoulder-length hair soaked to his scalp. His long bony jaws gripped a stubby cold cigar.

The blowing of the horses was as loud as escaping steam as Fargo drew back inside the coach.

The little drummer was speaking. "I hear they been having more than a few holdups in this part of the country. Lot of gold and silver moving about. Got to expect it. The Comstock's the Comstock, and it's got to attract the thieves and such."

"Holdups!" The little woman beside him seemed to draw into a knot of trepidation. "Bandits! My word!"

"They call them road agents, ma'am," the drummer said in a bland tone of voice.

Fargo again had that strange sense of something not right. His eyes were on the drummer as the crack of a pistol suddenly rang outside the coach, and a hard voice called for the driver to pull up.

184

The passengers were instantly thrown by the sudden reining of the horses. Fargo saw the drummer's spectacles fly out of his coat pocket, while he was himself thrown toward the girl beside him as the horses made a dash for the shoulder of the road. But Fargo hardly touched her, his bodily reactions so quick that he was off balance only a second. In a flash he had opened the opposite coach door, grabbed the girl by the wrist, and pulled her out onto the bank alongside the road.

Landing easily, he pulled her down behind a pair of boulders from where he had a good view of the arrested stagecoach and the man covering it with a leveled handgun from the other side of the road.

Meanwhile up on the box the driver was sawing leather as hard as he could, the great strands of the master reins coiled into the boot. The panicked horses were brought up on their haunches, half on top of the lead team and with the coach pushing the rumps of the pair of wheel horses.

The guard had pitched forward into the frantic horseflesh. Rolling free unhurt, he threw his hands high in the air.

"Throw out the box!"

It was another voice now, not the man with the gun. The new voice came from another spot along the road, up ahead of where the coach had halted and out of Fargo's view.

He was lying right on top of the girl, who, realizing her position, had started to squirm out from under him.

"Stop it!" he hissed. "Lie still till I see how many there are, and where."

"Get off me!"

"Don't move!" He put his big hand over her mouth, more aware now of the soft, mobile body beneath him, the slight but definite odor of her perfume. "Just be still."

"You get off me!" She almost spat the words, the brown eyes glaring furiously up at him.

"Sorry," he said. "Not a good time for getting to know you." And he pressed his suddenly hard member against her leg.

She had stopped struggling and lay rigid as iron beneath his big body, her legs clamped together, her eyes clenched shut in fury.

He raised himself slightly, moved carefully away, his eyes watching the man with the gun. The other man was still not visible. The man with the gun was tall, wearing a long duster coat and a beaver plug hat.

"Goddammit!" he barked. "Throw out that box! We know it's there."

"Think I'm loco?" cried the driver as he desperately sawed the reins. "You want them horses to pull this coach plumb over the hill?"

The Trailsman's eyes swept the terrain, then returned to take in detail. First the general picture of what confronted them, and then the details. Something he couldn't quite put his finger on was nagging him, but he didn't dwell on it. He knew it would come when the moment was appropriate.

They were lying to the far side of the coach, away from the man with the gun. The road was cut around a small knoll. On the east side the hill dropped away gently from the shoulder of the road, but on the west side the road had been blasted through a huge wall of rock. A number of great boulders still lay where they had fallen on that side. It was a good spot for a holdup, for any stage would have to slow to a walk before reaching the boulders, which afforded perfect cover for highwaymen.

Fargo watched the man with the gun motion to the guard. "You get the box."

The guard hurried to obey. He stood on the front wheel and reached into the boot.

"Hurry it!" snapped the voice of the man who was still out of sight.

"It weighs a ton," groaned the guard. But the order had given him extra strength. The box came out of the boot and toppled to the road with a crash.

"Line up the passengers," the same voice ordered.

Fargo lay absolutely still, listening to the girl's breathing. "You stay here," he whispered. "And don't move."

"Where are you going?" Her words speared him, demanding, still angry.

"I've got to find out how many they are, and where."

"But why not just let them have the box?" she said in a hard whisper. "Do you want to get us all killed?"

"That's a dumb question."

"They'll just let us go. All they want is the money."

"No, they won't let us go."

"Why? How do you know they won't?"

"They plan to kill us," he said evenly, and heard the sharp intake of her breath.

"But why? I don't understand."

"It's simple," he said quietly, his eyes still watching the road as he spoke softly to the girl. "The man up there isn't wearing a mask. And so he isn't figuring on any survivor recognizing him."

They were silent as Fargo watched the guard opening the door of the coach, accompanying this action with the quite unnecessary words, "It's a holdup."

The drummer and the little lady with the pointed nose descended to stand next to the guard facing the man with the gun.

Fargo had slipped to a fresh vantage point behind a big clump of sage; and now his eyes found the second road agent. The man was standing with a rifle in his hands in the shadow of one of the big boulders.

"You looking for someone?"

And Fargo realized the man with the rifle was speaking to one of the three lined up beside the coach, while the driver up on the box was still having a time gentling his horses.

It was the drummer who answered, his voice grainy in the wet air. "I was looking for your accomplice," he said. "The big fellow, the one they call the Trailsman. He's disappeared with one of the passengers. That's a neat trick having a plant right inside the coach." And the drummer coughed out a tight laugh.

"Damn!" Fargo swore as he raised himself to one knee and shot the man with the rifle in the throat. His target had not yet hit the ground before the Trailsman had thrown himself behind a pile of rocks, snapping a second shot at the first bandit, who had fired wildly in his direction and missed. Fargo's next shot was true, the big Colt .45 pumping lead into the bandit's belly and shattering his spine. He collapsed like a red, wet rag. It was over in seconds, the two highwaymen lying prone in death, while the driver fought wildly to control his spooked horses and the passengers and guard stared in shock.

"Don't anybody move!" Fargo's words cut hard into the grim tableau as he instantly slipped to a fresh cover, just in case there were others in the holdup.

His eyes covered the terrain carefully. He could see the girl lying where he had left her, the passengers and guard starting to fidget, and the driver finally settling the horses. He waited, looking twice at everything, trying to see in depth, to project himself into what he was looking at. And he was aware once more of the strange dissatisfaction, the feeling that there was something there that he was not seeing. And then, as he stepped out into full view, he remembered.

"Seems to be just the two of them," he said casually.

"Well, you sure surprised me, Trailsman." It was the drummer. "Like you likely heard, I thought you were their accomplice, figured they'd planted you with us passengers for insurance." A pale grin came into the pasty face. "Sure glad I was wrong, and I thank you for saving us."

Fargo's eyes had never left the drummer's face and hands, and he noted how small and very white those hands were. He dropped the big Colt back into its holster. His hand dropped to his side, and he started to turn away.

The round little man was fast, the derringer appearing out of nowhere into his small white hand. But the Trailsman had never taken his attention away from the drummer, and he was faster. The Colt was out and up and the drummer was falling, it seemed, even before the report crashed into the countryside. Fargo had shot him right between the eyes, blowing his head apart.

The girl, who had come up to where Fargo was standing, barely stifled a scream. The little middle-aged woman didn't. She shrieked and then started to swear, her lips trembled, her whole body shook. She started to babble.

"Handle her," Fargo ordered the girl.

"What did you shoot him for?" The brown eyes stared at the drummer's body in shock and dismay. "Are you crazy? He wasn't doing anything!"

Fargo was reloading the Colt. His voice was calm as he said, "He was looking for the accomplice. Well, he found him."

"What do you mean!" The girl had slipped her arm around the other woman, who was sobbing. "What do you mean?" she repeated. "Maybe you're one of the gang like he said!"

A grim smile touched the corners of the big man's mouth. "They had him planted in the coach—just in case anything went wrong. I was what went wrong, so he tipped them off. You heard him. If you want to turn him over, you'll see the hideout gun he pulled."

"And he'd of sure taken all that loot," the driver

cut in from the box, and released a long, low whistle.

"But how did you know?" the girl asked, her eyes still staring with shock at the swift violence of the three killings. And then her anger moved her toward a stronger control. "You seemed to know it all in advance, damn you!"

"You'll maybe see his glasses on the floor of the coach where he dropped them," Fargo said mildly.

"Glasses? Spectacles?"

"Except the lenses are tinted blue. Drummers don't wear blue-tinted glasses, but cardsharps do. They use them to spot the marks on the backs of cards. He was also carrying that derringer in a special arm holdout. Anything else you want to know?"

By now the older woman had calmed down and was again rational, though still crying softly. The girl still had her arm around her and seemed to have forgotten her own sense of shock and anger in her concern for her companion. After the two of them had climbed back into the coach, Fargo and the guard loaded the box back into the boot.

The driver released the taut reins. The horses heaved forward, and with a heavy pull he guided them back onto the road. As the teams crested the hill and surged into a gallop, the guard swung up on the rear of the coach and made his way to his place beside the driver. Fargo, who was already atop the swaying coach, leaned down, opening the door below, and then easily swung inside to the amazement of the two female passengers.

There was an expectant crowd waiting for the

stage as it drove into Virginia City and pulled up at the stage office.

"We owe you our thanks," the girl said coolly as Fargo opened the door for her.

"Anytime." He grinned. "Might look you up. I plan to be in town a short spell."

Her face was totally without expression as she said, "I don't believe my husband would care for that."

"I wasn't intending to invite him along," Fargo replied easily.

"*I* don't care for it!"

And with her lips pressed together she stepped down from the coach, leaving Fargo with the slight scent of hyacinth and the vision of a superb rear end. His eyes followed her as he moved now to the outside of the crowd and watched her being greeted by a redheaded, sandy-looking man of about thirty. He could only see her back, but he caught something of her rigidity even so as she offered her cheek for her escort to kiss. Her husband? Whoever it was, Fargo could clearly see that the girl was not boiling over for him. Maybe he would see her again. The big man with the lake-blue eyes had an idea he definitely would.